The Neighbor's Daughter

A Mystery

Faraz Ahmed

To my Aunt, Noshaba, who gave me the gift of my first book on my 8th birthday.
To my mom and dad, both of whom never denied me from purchasing books despite the money being tight.
To my sister, Murk, who introduced me to the Harry Potter series, which changed my life by making me seriously interested in writing fiction.
To my daughter, Maheen, who loves reading stories and inspired me to write this one.

Contents

Chapter One

John Ferris stared at the house at the end of the street in disbelief, his car's engine still idling. He checked the address he had scribbled on the Post-it Note one last time. Double-checked it with the numbers on the mailbox, which stood slightly askew in a yellowed patch of overgrown lawn. He shook his head and killed the engine.

John Ferris stepped out of the car, pulled up his coat collar against the cool fall wind, and surveyed the house he'd call home for the next few weeks. It was a two-story structure, like the rest of the homes on the avenue. The exterior of the house consisted of rust-colored brick on the bottom floor, and pea-soup green vinyl siding cladding the upper level. It had a gray asphalt shingle roof that glowed blue, backlit by the late fall sun low above the horizon. The architectural style (if there was one to speak of) was a hybrid between that of a ranch-style barn house and a mid-century modern bungalow. John Ferris chuckled and shook his head—the places he had to go to earn an honest buck!

It would be a temporary arrangement, John reminded himself as he took his suitcase and briefcase out of the trunk. When he slammed the trunk shut, John couldn't help but notice that here, at the end of the street, there was only one other house, separated from his temporary lodging by a faded picket fence with a few wooden boards missing. The next-door neighbor's home was about the same shape and size as his but slightly less shabby. The two houses sat quite a decent distance away from the rest of the homes on the upper end of the street. Detached, cut off as if a tornado had ripped through, clearing everything in its path and no one dared challenge the resulting demarcation.

Just as well, John thought. He wasn't in much of a neighborly mood these days. He needed peace and quiet to concentrate on his work. The last thing he wanted was bands of kids making a racket at all hours of the day with skateboards and bicycles and whatever it was they used nowadays to irritate people.

He rolled his suitcase up the concrete path to the front door and stopped cold. A ragged doll lay on the pavement. John could have easily stepped over it. Instead, he looked left and right to make sure no one was watching, then kicked the doll sending it in a high arc into his neighbor's yard. Right on cue, John detected movement in an upstairs window of his neighbor's house. He glanced up and saw the curtains swaying behind the closed glass pane.

Way to go, John!

He hurried for the front door, half expecting his neighbor to come out and give him an earful. The property manager, Mr. Samuel Wakefield (who must have had a two-pack-a-day smoking habit judging from his telephone voice), told John he would hide the front door key under a clay statue of a crying angel the last time they spoke. And sure enough, there it was.

John entered the house and locked the door behind him. He paused to look around. The furniture was so old it was almost cool, in a 1970s sitcom kind of way. He walked through the foyer, past the living room, and entered the kitchen. He propped his suitcase against the wall, set his briefcase on the dining table, and decided to take a little tour of the place.

The downstairs consisted of the usual living areas and a single large bedroom with an en suite bathroom. That's where he would sleep.

For the hell of it, he went upstairs to take a peek. There were three more bedrooms, smaller than the one downstairs, connected by a dark corridor with lime-green wall-to-wall carpeting. John looked out an upstairs window that opened onto the backyard. In the distance were a fallow field and a thick line of oaks behind it.

John was thinking how he'd never have to come upstairs. It would spare him the sight of that lime-green carpet. As he inspected the upstairs bathroom, the doorbell rang. He was momentarily stunned, as can be expected when one hears an unfamiliar chime for the first time. Figuring it must be Mr. Wakefield, the property manager, coming to check on things, John quickly headed downstairs.

When he opened the door, he was surprised to see a man and a woman standing on the concrete stoop. They appeared to be in their late thirties or early forties but had a worn look about them. The woman had thyroid eyes with thick veins radiating out from the pupils. The man wore thick glasses and sported a caramel walrus mustache.

They emitted an anachronistic vibe. The clothes they wore, their hairstyles, seemed straight out of a theater costume department. The man gazed at John with a broad grin, whereas the woman seemed poised to cry at the slightest provocation. She stood stiffly, holding a dish covered in aluminum foil.

John regained his bearings after the initial shock and said, "Can I help you?"

The man said, "Hello neighbor," in a high-pitched gleeful voice. "We saw you pull up, and we thought we'd come and introduce ourselves." The man enunciated every syllable in the manner of a radio preacher.

"Oh," John said. "You live next door?"

The man chuckled. "We most certainly do. My name is Ted. Ted Noland."

John shook his hand. "John Ferris. Nice to meet you."

"And this is my wife, Mary-Beth. And the little one's name is Sarah."

John had a moment of hesitation. He didn't know whether he should shake the wife's hand, which would have been impossible with both her hands occupied. He didn't want to appear rude, yet something told him it would be inappropriate to shake the woman's hand. Mary-Beth Noland resolved the issue by handing the dish to her husband and clasping John's hand loosely.

Ted Noland said, "Sarah, dear, won't you be a big girl and say hello to Mr. Ferris?"

Due to the minor handshake snafu, John had momentarily forgotten about their daughter. He looked down but didn't see her. Thinking she might be hiding behind Mrs. Noland's skirt, he tried to angle his neck to look behind her.

"Is she here?" John asked.

"She's a shy one," Ted Noland said with a wink.

For a moment, John Ferris thought he might be the target of a practical joke. A camera operator might be hiding in the bushes filming his reaction to the farce. In days, the video would be all over the internet. He quickly dismissed the notion, and it dawned on him that the Nolands were on the nuttier side of eccentric.

"Her name is Sarah?" John asked.

"Sarah Elizabeth Noland, just like her gran-gran," Ted Noland said. "Sarah, sweetheart, tell the nice man how old you are."

There was only silence. John's eyes widened slightly, and he rolled his lips inward, not sure what to say or whether to say anything at all. After what felt like an eternity, John Ferris said, "I guess she's a shy one."

"She sure is," Ted said. Mary-Beth Noland tried to smile. She abruptly looked at her feet when her attempt failed.

"Are you sure she's here?" John said, not wanting to participate in a shared delusion.

"Why, of course, she's here," Ted said. His smile faded. "She's standing right there." He pointed to a spot beside Mary-Beth, his eyes remaining locked with John's.

John stood impassive.

Ted looked at the spot where he was pointing. "Well, jeepers-creepers, she was standing there just a minute ago." With a puzzled look on his face, he said, "She must have run back to the house." His smile resurfaced. "That's it. She ran back to the house. She's a little firecracker, she is."

Mary-Beth let out a nervous laugh and looked down again.

These people are nuts, John told himself, a couple of pistons short of a V-8. To defuse the tension, he said, "I'm sure I'll meet her, sooner or later."

"I see you're married," Ted said, pointing at the ring on John's finger. "Do you have children? It would be so nice for Sarah to have someone to play with."

"Oh, no. No children."

"That's too bad," a deflated Ted Noland said.

"I'm not moving here permanently. I'm just renting the house for a few weeks. For work."

"I mean, it's too bad you don't have kids," Ted Noland said. "I couldn't imagine life without our little Sarah. We men are all the same. When we're single, we think we know precisely what we want. But let me tell you, Mr. Ferris; until you hold your baby for the first time, until you see those tiny eyes looking back at you, your spirit is not complete. And then, the first time you see your baby, in one instant, all your doubts wash away. And you realize, deep in your heart, you will never be complete again if not through your child."

John shifted his weight and tried not to squirm. "Like I said. I'm just here on a short-term assignment."

"That's really too bad. We were thrilled at the thought of having new neighbors. Weren't we, mother?" Mary-Beth nodded vigorously. "We brought you a housewarming present." Ted passed the dish over to John, who took it reluctantly. "They're store-bought cookies. We didn't know you were coming; otherwise, Mary-Beth would have baked you a peach cobbler."

"There's no need for you to go through all that trouble. I'm here by myself and—"

"Our Sarah just loves her peach cobbler. She can't get enough of it."

"Is that right?"

"I know, Mary-Beth will make you a nice turkey and cheese casserole tomorrow. What do you say, Mr. Ferris?"

"Please, don't trouble yourselves. I have a full day at work tomorrow, and I'll probably go out to dinner with my associates."

Ted Noland wagged a finger at John. "Mr. Ferris, you know there's nothing better than a home-cooked meal."

There was only one way to get rid of these people. John heard himself say, "You're right. A turkey and cheese casserole would be great. Looking forward to it." John thanked his neighbors once more and casually backed into the house, closing the front door at the first chance he got.

He leaned back against the door, exhaled sharply, and shook his head.

He headed to the kitchen and plopped the dish on the kitchen counter when his cellphone rang. The caller ID lit up with a picture of his wife and the heading, Katie Ferris.

John picked up and said, "Hey, honey, I was just about to call you."

"I was starting to get worried."

"I'm sorry. I took a minute to stretch my legs, and just as I was about to call you, I got an unexpected visit from the next-door neighbors."

"That sounds nice," Katie said.

"They're crazy," John said. "And I don't mean peculiar. I mean certifiably insane."

Katie chuckled. "Come on, John. Loosen up a little. It's not Chicago. You're in a small town. People are folksier. It's not your Michigan Avenue crowd. This might be a good experience for you. It might make you a little less anti-social."

"Anti-social? Who are you calling anti-social? I'm anything but. Your husband is a regular people lover."

"Sure, you are," Katie said. "That's why you became an accountant."

"I love you. Isn't that enough?"

Katie hesitated. "I'll let you get settled in. I know you must be tired from the drive."

"How are you, Katie?" John asked.

Katie sighed. "Lonely."

There was a long pause. "I'll get this job done quickly. And then I'm never leaving you again."

Chapter Two

The Chicago accounting firm John Ferris worked for needed their top number cruncher to lead their DeKalb branch, some sixty miles west of the windy city, before the annual audit of a VIP client—one of the largest corn and seed suppliers of the Midwest. Dirksen Corn had engaged in creative bookkeeping for years. It was a rookie accountant in the DeKalb office who first noted the discrepancies, a young woman named Brenda Collins. Brenda calculated that, between fines, penalties, and unpaid interest on back taxes, Dirksen Corn stood to owe Uncle Sam upwards of ten million dollars. John Ferris, the miracle worker, was called in to mitigate the damage.

John got the call on Thanksgiving Day, just as his father-in-law was getting ready to carve the turkey. Three days later, John packed his suitcase and gave his wife a long embrace to say goodbye. Sometimes it sucked to be the best bean counter in the firm. The best in Chicago if you asked Katie Ferris.

With the holiday upon them, the office assistant couldn't secure temporary housing for John through the regular channels. It was sheer luck that a secretary at the DeKalb subsidiary knew of a house for rent in the town of Maple Park, some eight miles away. It was a four-bedroom house, much more square footage than John needed, but the firm was picking up the cost of rent and utilities. At the end of the day, it would be Dirksen Corn to foot the bill.

John knew that tomorrow, his first day at the DeKalb office, would be as hectic as they come. The first order of the day would be to meet with Brenda Collins and go over her numbers. Then, a short break to bang his head against a wall before pulling himself together, rolling his sleeves up, and getting down to work.

What he needed tonight was a good dinner, a hot shower, and a good night's sleep. A quick internet search revealed the town of Maple Park boasted not only one but two restaurants within blocks of each other. (The commercial part of town was a single street, after all). There was The Lodi Tap House and Casey's. John was sure he'd be visiting both in a matter of days. Tonight, he'd go to Lodi. That photograph on their website of a stacked juicy hamburger sure looked enticing after a long drive.

The place was empty for a Sunday night. A vintage Wurlitzer jukebox was playing country music, a song featuring a whiny slide guitar offset by the baritone voice of the singer. John's waitress was efficient and friendly without being flirtatious, a pleasant change from your typical Chicago eatery. And the burger was terrific. Yeah, he'd be back here for sure.

John polished off his food, overtipped the waitress, and headed home, where he took a long steamy shower. He got into a soft V-neck t-shirt and boxer shorts, set his cellphone alarm for six AM, and settled in bed.

He was feeling drained. It hadn't been the drive from Chicago, nor the strange meeting with the neighbors that was sapping him. It was the thought of what was to come. John had a name for it: anticipation fatigue. He fluffed his pillow, rolled onto his side, and closed his eyes. Within minutes, John was snoring softly, entering that deep, early dreamless stage of sleep. He was completely out when a crashing sound jolted him awake.

He sat up in bed, trying to get his bearings. It took him a moment to realize he wasn't in his bedroom in Chicago. Something about waking up in an unfamiliar setting caused his heart to start pounding.

John swung his legs over the edge of the bed and got to his feet quietly. The first thought that came to mind was that there was an intruder in the house. A thief, perhaps, expecting an empty home, trying to make an easy score. John stood in silence, his eyes adjusting to the darkness, before taking a couple of careful steps. He felt two things simultaneously: a sharp object under his foot and a cool breeze blowing through the room. Broken glass! Someone had smashed in the bedroom window.

John called out, "I got a gun!"

Wasn't that the standard thing to say in these situations?

The reply was a giggle. A high-pitched laugh, that of a girl. It was coming from outside the broken window, from the backyard.

Immediately John thought of the Nolands' daughter, Sarah. Ted Noland had called her a firecracker. A pain in the ass is what she was, pretending to meet the new neighbor before running off without her parents' consent. Who knows what else she might be capable of?

John grabbed his cell phone and turned on the flashlight app. He scanned the floor first. He saw pieces of broken glass fanning away from the window and a rock the size of a fist.

There was more girlish giggling.

John stepped toward the window in a careful heel-toe gait and shone the light out the hole into the backyard. There was no one there. He turned the beam left, then right, panning the entire yard. Nothing . . .

The little monster thought she was going to get away with this. She had no idea who she was dealing with. He was John

Ferris, a top-notch Chicago bookkeeper. A man who laughed in the face of accounting danger where lesser men faltered.

John pulled on a pair of sweatpants and ran for the front door barefoot. He swung the front door open so hard the knob smashed against the outdoor wall.

John ran out in an arc, encroaching onto his neighbor's lawn. He shone his cell phone light toward the backyard, tracked the beam back over a flowerbed, and fixed it on the front door.

I'll show you who's a firecracker!

John marched to the front door of the Noland house and rang the doorbell. When there was no reply, he pounded the door with his fist. A moment later, he heard footfalls inside the house.

John took a step back, got into a wide stance, and crossed his arms. The door opened. Mary-Beth stood at the entrance in a terry cloth night robe, looking even more ghostly than she had earlier that day.

"Good evening!" John said emphatically.

"Can I help you?" Mary-Beth said. She asked the question all innocent-like. As though John had come over to place a complaint concerning the store-bought cookies she had brought him.

"Where is she?" John said.

"I'm sorry?"

"You heard me. Where is she?"

Mary-Beth's expression shifted from confusion to a look of annoyance. "What do you want from us?"

"I'm looking for Sarah. I'd like to have a word with your daughter and your husband if you don't mind," John said.

Mary-Beth's eyes widened. Her mouth dropped open. This was no longer a look of annoyance. It was utter terror.

Mary-Beth wailed, "Go away! Leave us alone! Just go away!"

Mary-Beth's reaction took John by surprise. He stood there speechless as she slammed the door in his face. When the shock of her reaction wore off, John scowled. He lifted his fist again, ready to knock the blasted door down, then stopped himself.

He looked at the clock on his cell phone. It read 10:05 p.m. There was nothing he'd accomplish tonight. And tomorrow was going to be a long day. The best thing he could do was to go to sleep in an upstairs bedroom, come back in the morning, and talk to Ted Noland with a cooler head.

As he crossed the dew-soaked grass in bare feet, John muttered to himself, "I'm never having kids if it's the last thing I do."

Chapter Three

John Ferris lay in bed for hours, staring at the vaulted ceiling of one of the upstairs bedrooms, unable to sleep. He recounted the events of the previous evening, trying to make some logical sense of the ordeal. Unfortunately, human nature was not as rational and well-ordered as accounting. There was no precise double-entry system to guide people's motivation, no tidy columns where you could add up human behavior so that it made sense.

Ted and Mary-Beth Noland had baffled him. Even worse, they had succeeded at touching a raw nerve in John. Unwittingly, they had found a pinch point, reviving a part of his past he had tried so hard to bury.

John finally fell asleep in the predawn hours. His closed eyes twitched to fitful dreams, and his body jerked awake at the sound of the alarm on his cell phone at 6 a.m.

He sat up, rubbed the sleep out of his eyes, and headed for the shower. After getting dressed, John ventured into the garage and found a folded moving box. A half-used roll of duct tape sat atop a can of varnish. He grabbed that too and went to the kitchen.

He cut a square of cardboard from the moving box using a steak knife. Then, he tore strips of duct tape to fasten the patch he made over the hole in the downstairs bedroom window. It was a crappy fix, but it would block the wind if nothing else. He'd put in a service call to Samuel Wakefield later in the day.

Now, it was time for a friendly chat with Ted Noland.

John walked out the front door and marched across the yellow front lawn. He was glad to see Ted, standing next to a flower bed, hand-watering some tiny plants that looked like they had no chance to bloom. Ted had his back turned and hadn't noticed John approaching.

John cleared his voice and said, "Good morning, Ted."

Ted turned abruptly with the water can still angled downward, spilling water on his shoes. "Oh! Good morning, neighbor. Did you sleep well?"

Ted Noland looked serene, oblivious. His blank expression showed no sign of the previous night's tumult. It was as though someone had unplugged Ted's mind while he slept and done a hard reboot.

John put his hands on his hips. "Actually, that's what I came to talk to you about. I didn't sleep very well at all."

Ted gave John an understanding look. "That's not unusual, John. First night in a strange house. I know where you're coming from. I never get as much as a wink in a hotel. Yessir, I'll take my eight-year-old mattress over any other bed any day of the week, hands down!"

"It wasn't the mattress, Ted. It was your daughter."

"Now wait a minute . . ."

"She threw a rock through my window last night. Did Mary-Beth tell you?"

Ted let out a nervous chuckle. "That's impossible. My Sarah would never do anything like that."

"You want to see for yourself? Be my guest. There's a hole in my window, broken glass on my floor, and a rock that looks like it came from the edge of your flower bed."

"That's a preposterous allegation, John. Why would a little girl throw a rock through your window?"

"I don't know. Let's go ask her."

John took a step toward the Noland house front door. Ted moved in front of him, blocking his way. "No. I can't let you do that."

"Why not?"

"She's still fast asleep."

"Let's wake her up."

Ted's expression grew stern. "Listen, John. I'm sorry about your window. I really am. But Sarah had nothing to do with it. Now, if you try to barge into my house, I'll have no choice but to call the sheriff. Do you understand?"

John put his hands in his pockets. "Yeah, I understand." He leaned into Ted until their noses were separated by inches and said, "I'll tell you what, Ted. I'll call the sheriff myself. As soon as I get back from work."

John turned on his heels and walked back to his house. A faint smile surfaced on Ted's face, who raised his hand in a tentative wave and called out, "Have a nice day!"

***

Ted Noland was nowhere to be seen when John left the house to go to work. Neither was his wife or daughter. Just as well, John thought. He'd have a long day at work and didn't need another confrontation that might make him late. What he did need was coffee, plenty of it, and strong.

John headed down Maple Park's main street and spotted a convenience store with shuttered-up gas pumps in the front. He pulled into a parking spot and went into the store. John found the breakfast corner: stacks of Styrofoam cups on a counter with stained air pots. He filled a large cup and looked at the pastry choices. There was a tray of cinnamon rolls glazed with enough sugar to send the entire population of

Maple Park into a diabetic coma for a week. John opted for an overbaked bran muffin that looked like it had come out of a cement mixer.

The cashier was a pert red-headed young woman in her early twenties with freckles, a round chin, and a pleasant smile. She was slender, but there was something disproportionate about her body. The plastic name tag on her blue work vest read, Emily. She rang John up and read out his total in a cheerful voice.

As John pulled cash out of his billfold, the store clerk asked him, "Passing through?"

The question caught John off guard. No one would ever ask such a thing in Chicago. But out here in the country, such queries weren't considered intrusive. She was simply being friendly.

"Not quite," John said. "I'm here for work. I'll be in Maple Park for a few weeks."

"In that case, welcome to town. Please keep us in mind for all your shopping needs. We have canned goods, frozen pizza, a fabulous dairy section, and the best selection of beer in town."

"Really?" John tried to sound impressed.

"To be honest," Emily said, "we're the only place that sells beer in town, outside of the restaurants and taverns."

"I guess that makes you the best," John said.

Emily smiled bashfully and blushed a little. "Yeah, I guess you can say that."

"Well, Emily, I'll be sure to keep you in mind for all my dairy and frozen pizza needs, and whatever else comes up. You have yourself a lovely day."

Emily looked away, pretended to wipe something off her cash register, and said, "You too."

At the DeKalb accounting office, the manager welcomed John warmly and introduced him to Brenda Collins, a young woman in an off-the-rack pantsuit and intense blue eyes. Brenda gave John a two-grip handshake, a gesture someone in a college class must have taught her projected earnestness. She led him to a conference room where a dozen bankers' boxes sat on a pine veneer table.

They sat down across from each other, and John outlined the strategy they'd employ to prepare for their client's audit. "We can reclassify certain expenses, but only if there's a legitimate basis. We may be representing Dirksen Corn's interests, but not at the cost of our firm's reputation. Everything has to be done strictly by the book."

Brenda was a quick study. After a brief rough patch, she was off to the races. By noon, the two of them had accomplished more than John had hoped for. But he knew this was a marathon, not a sprint. There was a ton more work to do. At 12:30, John suggested they take a break and invited Brenda to lunch at a diner across the street.

The diner catered to a mix of office workers and middle managers. John and Brenda sat down in a booth by the window. John ordered a turkey club sandwich, hold the mayo, Brenda a Reuben on rye. They both drank iced tea.

As they were waiting for their food, John asked Brenda, "Where'd you go to college?"

Brenda said, "Peoria. That's where my family's from."

"What brings you to DeKalb?"

"My husband. We met in college and got married a week after graduation."

"That's great," John said, trying to keep the conversation polite and nonchalant.

"I see you're married too," Brenda said, glancing at his ring finger. "How long?"

"We just celebrated our twelfth anniversary."

"Congratulations!" Brenda said with a sincere smile. Then came the rub. "Do you have any kids?"

John tried to dismiss the query quickly. "Nah," he said and took a long sip from the straw in his iced tea.

"How come?" Brenda questioned. She was trying to hold that smile, but the corners of her lips were betraying her.

John was about to give his usual perfunctory answer but sensed it wouldn't fly with Brenda Collins, the up-and-coming accountant whose keen eye spotted the discrepancies with the Dirksen Corn account.

"It's like this," John said in an even tone. "Many people go through life doing things in a particular sequence because that's what everyone else does. Go to college, get a job, get married, buy a house in the suburbs, get a minivan, maybe a boat to sail Lake Michigan on the weekends. They don't even question if these are the right choices for them. They just bow to conformity. Well, I don't want to submit to any cultural standards. I'm my own man."

Brenda tilted her head. "And your wife is fine with that?"

John looked away. "Oh, yeah. She doesn't care for boats or minivans."

Brenda scoffed. "What a load of horse manure."

"I beg your pardon?"

"Not bowing to conformity—what a bunch of bull. It sounds to me like you're scared."

"Of what?"

Brenda took a sip of iced tea and shrugged. "I don't know. You tell me."

The waitress arrived with their lunch. She deposited the plates on the table, asked if they needed more iced tea, and when they assured her they didn't, told them to enjoy their sandwiches. The interruption allowed John to duck the question. At least for a little while.

Brenda took a bite of her sandwich, used a paper napkin to wipe her lips, and said, "Tell me, what are you scared of?"

It was time for John to try a different tack. "Have you ever done a formal accounting analysis of what it costs to raise a child nowadays? To start, you have health care expenses for maternity care, obstetrics, and some eighteen years of pediatrician visits, immunizations, braces, and (*God forbid!*) drug rehab. Throw in food and clothing, educational expenses—I don't have to remind you of the cost of college education, do

I?—transportation costs, toys, computers, cell phones; it never ends! I mean, we're talking well over a million dollars per child. And that's without taking into account the opportunity costs. If you were to invest that money in a mutual fund with a seven percent return compounded annually over the life of—"

"My husband and I have been trying to get pregnant. We can't. Or I should say, I can't. We went to a fertility clinic, but the doctor told us there's no chance."

John froze. In a soft voice, he said, "I'm sorry to hear that."

Brenda sighed. "It was quite a blow. We always imagined ourselves raising little ones. Ironic, isn't it? The one thing I really wanted is beyond my reach."

"There's always adoption," John said.

"Yes. We're looking into it."

John took a bite of his sandwich and chewed slowly.

Brenda waited for a beat before saying, "The last time I checked, it's not a crime to dislike children."

John swallowed and said, "It's just that they constantly cry and seep bodily fluids from every orifice."

"So, it's babies that frighten you?"

"And the older kids too. I don't know how to talk to them. I can't even have a conversation about baseball with a kid. Can you imagine me talking about, you know, those big conversations fathers are supposed to have with their sons?"

Brenda smiled wistfully. "Were you an only child?"

John took another bite of his sandwich, chewed thoroughly, and swallowed before answering, "Yes, I was."

Brenda nodded. "I guess that explains it. I understand your choice," she said, "I even respect it. But I think you're making parenthood into something much scarier than it really is."

The waitress was walking by. John took advantage of the moment to turn and ask for the check.

Chapter Four

The sky was turning dark when John Ferris left the office for the day. Thunderclouds towered high above the horizon. He felt exhausted as he left the office for the day but satisfied. Thanks to Brenda's proficiency, they had accomplished more than John had hoped. After lunch, they pressed their noses to the grindstone and went through an entire box of documents without a further word on the subject of children or parenthood.

John climbed into his car and started driving home. He thought he'd better stop at Maple Park's best and only convenience store to pick up a carton of milk, a box of cereal, a few cans of soup, and a frozen pizza.

When he stepped into the store, he was surprised to see Emily, the store clerk, crouched on her knees, restocking a shelf of candy.

"You're still here?" John said.

"And you're back," Emily said.

"You've had a long day. Haven't you?"

Emily shrugged as she got to her feet. "I'm used to it. Anyway, there's nothing better to do in this town."

"Well, if you need a good accountant to help you with all the money you're earning, please keep me in mind."

Emily smiled. "Wouldn't that be nice! Are you looking for any items in particular tonight?"

John grabbed a basket and said, "I'm just going to grab a few things. Thanks."

"I'll be at the cash register, then."

As John grabbed a carton of milk out of the refrigerated display case, he started thinking. There was only one convenience store in town and (from what he had seen so far) only one store clerk. He reached for a box of cereal that didn't feature a cartoon character on its label and put it in his basket.

Emily seemed like a bright and observant young lady. What light could she shed on his new neighbors, Ted and Mary-Beth Noland? He found the soup aisle, piled a few cans of chicken noodles in his basket, and headed for the cash register.

"Will that do it for you?" Emily asked.

John was debating how to bring up the subject of the Nolands when he realized he had forgotten something. He slapped his forehead and said, "Frozen pizza! I'll be right back."

"No rush," Emily said.

John reached into the freezer, grabbed a thin-crust meat-lovers supreme and told himself, just ask her. It's no big deal.

Emily said, "That's my favorite," as John placed the pizza box on the checkout counter.

"Did I tell you about my neighbors? The Nolands. Ted and Mary-Beth, and their daughter Sarah. Do you know them?"

"Oh, sure. The Nolands shop here all the time."

"That's what I figured," John said, nodding repeatedly. "Good people."

"Oh, yeah," Emily said. "They're sweet."

"They brought me cookies last night."

"Is that right? That was thoughtful."

"Yeah," John said, "store-bought, but it's the thought that counts."

Emily covered her mouth to stifle a laugh. "I bet they purchased those cookies here."

"They're regulars, are they?" John asked.

"Oh, sure. They come here all the time."

"So, you know them?"

Emily shrugged. "It's a small town."

"What do you think of their daughter, Sarah?"

"I have never met her," Emily said as she bagged John's groceries.

"You have never met her?" Emily shook her head. "Not even once? I thought they were regulars."

"Ted and Mary-Beth are. But they never bring their daughter along."

John wrinkled his brow. "Isn't that odd?"

Emily looked around. She leaned over the counter and whispered, "If you ask me, I think they're a little odd."

***

Lights were shining in the downstairs windows of the Noland home, but all the curtains were drawn. The upstairs was completely dark. John Ferris wouldn't waste his time on another useless conversation with Ted Noland. He parked his car, entered his home, tossed his briefcase onto the kitchen counter, and pulled out his smartphone. He looked up the number for the local sheriff's department and dialed it.

Forty minutes later, there was a knock at the door. John checked his wristwatch and went to open the front door. On the stoop was a uniformed man with closely cropped gray hair and a body like a heavy-weight boxer. He stood with his thumbs hooked on his glossy black belt, his holstered sidearm off to the side.

The man spoke in a matter-of-fact voice as if he were there to deliver flowers. "I'm Sheriff Brad Thornsby. I understand there's been some sort of a disturbance here."

"Please come in," John said. The sheriff entered, and John closed the door behind him. "Thanks for coming. Do you mind following me?"

The sheriff grunted.

John took him to the bedroom with the shattered window. He showed the sheriff the broken glass on the floor and re-moved the square of cardboard he had duct-taped to the pane earlier that morning. He explained what happened the night before, pointing to the rock on the floor at the salient moment.

The sheriff said, "Mmm. The fact that the broken glass is on the interior of the house tells me the rock was thrown in from the exterior."

John looked at the man, dumbfounded. "Well, yeah, I just told you that."

"You'd be surprised how many calls we get where some-one claims a rock was thrown through their window, but the shards of glass are outside."

"You're kidding," John said.

"Happens all the time. You said this happened around 10 p.m. last night?"

"That's right."

"And you heard a little girl laughing?"

"It was more like giggling."

"Did you happen to see the little girl?"

John said, "No. I mean, by the time I looked out the window, she was gone."

"So, you can't be absolute one-hundred percent sure the perpetrator was . . . a little girl."

"What, you don't believe me?"

The sheriff scratched his head. "I'm just wondering, what's a little girl doing outdoors at 10 p.m. throwing rocks into people's windows?"

"I don't know," John said. "Why don't we ask the next-door neighbors?"

Sheriff Thornsby raised both hands, palms forward. "Now, hold on a minute before you make false accusations. I understand you're not from around here."

John shot the sheriff a puzzled look. "What does that have to do with anything?"

"Look, you've got to understand something, this is not Chicago. There's no rampant crime here, vandalism and such. It's a sleepy little town. People look after each other. And when there's a little misunderstanding, a minor neighborly dispute, folks talk it out and seal the deal with a handshake."

"So, you're going to do nothing."

"What do you expect me to do? Get forensics out here to fingerprint a rock and run it through our national database of giggling girls? Mr. Ferris, I understand you're upset. I do. But I suggest you make a friendly call to your neighbor's house in the morning and iron things out man to man. If there's any more trouble," the sheriff reached into his shirt's breast pocket and pulled out a business card, "give us a call. In the meantime, you have yourself a blessed evening."

John followed the sheriff as he slowly walked through the house, taking an eyeful of the rooms he crossed, looking for who knows what. After letting the officer out, John looked out the window to see if the sheriff would pay the Noland's a visit.

He didn't. He got into his patrol car and coasted out of the neighborhood.

John cursed under his breath. He thought about it a minute and decided the best thing was to forget about the entire sordid incident. The run-in with Ted Noland wasn't an attack on his manhood or his pride. And if Brenda kept up the excellent work at the office, he'd be back in Chicago in no time. The Nolands were not worth fretting over.

John went to the kitchen, popped the frozen pizza in the oven, and phoned the property manager, Samuel Wakefield.

"A broken window? You've only been there one night!" Sam Wakefield said when John explained the situation.

"Do you think you can send someone in the morning to replace it?" John asked.

"Sure, I can. But a window ain't cheap."

"Just send the invoice to my company, and they'll pay for it." Another item to add to the Dirksen Corn account, John figured.

"How'd you manage to break a window so fast?" Mr. Wakefield asked.

"It's the craziest thing," John said. "The next-door neighbor's daughter flung a rock through it at 10 p.m. last night."

"That can't be. Who lets a little girl out after dark?"

John said, "I'm no expert on parenting matters, but I agree with you. At a minimum, it shows a blatant disregard for parental duties. The word neglect comes to mind."

"It couldn't have been the Nolands' daughter. She's only what . . . eight, nine years old? Must have been one of the older kids from up the street."

"What makes you so sure it couldn't have been Sarah Noland?"

Wakefield seemed to be holding something back. Finally, he said, "She's sickly, isn't she?"

"What do you mean?"

"I must have been to the house a hundred times over the years. There's always something to fix in an old place. Not once have I seen that little girl playing outside. So, I figured she's gotta be a little sickly. You know?"

John said, "She didn't seem sick last night. She seemed as strong as an ox. The way she launched that rock, she could be a backup pitcher for the Chicago Cubs. And then she laughed about it. And before I could get to the window, she was gone. A natural-born sprinter she is."

"You know something? My missus and I watched a TV show some time back about a little kid who couldn't go out in the sun cause his skin would blister up. The kid could only play outside at night. They called him the vampire boy or something like that. Maybe this little girl's the same way."

"Oh, she's a little monster, all right," John said. He thanked Mr. Wakefield for his time, waited for his pizza to finish cooking, and sat down to a miserable dinner alone.

Chapter Five

John Ferris sat up on the living room sofa, lowered the volume of the television set, and dialed his wife's phone number. She picked up immediately. It was apparent that she had been waiting for his call.

John said, "Hi, honey. What are you doing?"

"Getting ready for bed."

John looked at his wristwatch. "It's only eight-thirty."

"I have to be at the office early tomorrow. The grant application I'm working on is due next week, and large chunks of it have to be rewritten."

"Sounds exhilarating," John said sarcastically.

"Almost as exciting as double-entry accounting," Katie said.

"Don't knock double-entry accounting. Some historians think it was the single most important innovation that led to the European Renaissance."

"Yeah. So, you've told me. Many times."

John chuckled. "I miss you, Katie."

"How are things coming along with your kooky neighbors?" Katie asked.

"Well, let's see. Their daughter tossed a rock through my window last night," John said nonchalantly.

"What? That can't be right," Katie said.

"Want me to text you a picture of the broken glass? A guy is coming out to fix the window in the morning."

Katie's tone turned business-like, as it always did when she tried to resolve perplexing issues. "John, you're telling me that you witnessed a little girl throw a rock through your window."

John switched the phone to his other hand. "Well, I couldn't see her, could I? It was pitch black outside."

"At what time did this happen?"

John paused. He knew Katie would interrogate him with the doggedness of a hardened detective. He'd have to watch every word he uttered. "It was 10 p.m."

"But you didn't actually see your neighbor's daughter throw a rock through your window. What makes you think it was her?"

"I heard giggling. The unmistakable giggling of a little girl," John said with the satisfaction of a prosecutor presenting the smoking-gun evidence in front of a crowded courtroom.

Katie paused a moment. "It could have been anyone."

"Anyone who giggles like a little girl, I suppose," John rebutted, feeling he had gained the upper hand.

Katie regrouped. "Okay, John Ferris, assuming you did hear some form of giggling . . ."

"What am I, hallucinating now?"

"And granting the questionable deduction that any giggling you might have heard originated from a little girl, that still doesn't implicate your neighbor's daughter with absolute certainty."

John rubbed his brow. "How many little girls do you think run around at night in this neighborhood, smashing in people's windows as they sleep?"

"Did you talk to your neighbors about it?" Katie asked.

"I sure did," John said.

"And?"

"The woman went ballistic. She completely lost her marbles and started yelling at me. And the husband walked around this morning acting like he had just had a prefrontal lobotomy."

"What about the little girl? Did she have anything to say for herself?"

John chuckled. "That's the crazy thing. I have yet to see her. In fact, it seems like no one around here ever sees her. Not the clerk at the convenience store, not the property manager, not the sheriff . . ."

"The sheriff?" Katie questioned, her voice shooting up an octave.

"Yeah, I forgot to tell you. I called the sheriff to report the incident."

John heard Katie sigh a long sigh of disapproval.

Katie said, "You've only been there around twenty-four hours, and you already called the cops on your new neighbors?"

Feeling a little hurt, John said, "You make it sound like I have a habit of doing so. As if this is all my fault."

"John, honey, I really need to get some rest. Do yourself a favor: avoid these neighbors. They do sound a little eccentric. People like that can be unpredictable. The less contact you have with them, the less likely the situation will escalate. Just forget about the incident and let the whole thing blow over."

John replied, "That's fine with me, as long as they keep their little girl—"

"John?" Katie interrupted him. "Just let it go."

***

John found a broom and a dustpan tucked away in a kitchen closet. He walked into the downstairs bedroom and swept the broken glass off the floor. He had already replaced the cardboard patch on the broken window with fresh strips of duct tape. Tomorrow the window would be repaired to eliminate the last sign of the petty drama.

Katie was right. He had to forget the whole thing and not let it bother him. It would be easier to do once everything returned to its original condition. Some people had the irrational tendency to get stuck in a loop of echoing lament, replaying unfortunate episodes over and over, evoking the same painful feelings in a ring of torment. The key, John knew, was to eliminate visual stimuli that kept those thoughts alive. It was a lesson his parents had taught him at a very young age.

Satisfied with his work, John returned to the living room and watched the evening news. When his eyes grew heavy, he got up, brushed his teeth, and went to bed.

A westerly wind had picked up that evening. As John lay in bed, he could hear the rustling of leaves from the backyard oaks. There was a faint rapping of branches on the roof tiles that had an oddly soothing quality. It brought up memories of cozy fireplaces, hot cocoa, and freshly baked cinnamon cookies. He closed his eyes and could almost smell the rich aroma of stew and apple pie wafting from the kitchen of his childhood home, the scratchy sound of a Chopin sonata coming from his father's record player, his mother's voice calling from the kitchen, the patter of feet, the sound of laughter . . . a little girl laughing.

John's eyes shot open. His ears perked. He thought he heard some giggling. Then a scraping sound. Was it a branch rubbing on the eaves of the roof? No. It sounded much closer. It sounded like it was coming from the window.

John quickly turned on his bedside lamp. A triangle of light illuminated the bottom third of the bedroom. The window was a black slab, but the cardboard patch lit up with an eerie glow. The scratching sound resumed, louder than before, and as John looked on, four raised ridges appeared on the top end of the cardboard, spreading downward like narrow wheals on delicate flesh.

John shouted out, "Hey! Knock it off!"

The scratching ceased abruptly. The ridges stopped spreading. There was a burst of giggles that gave John gooseflesh. As his ears widened, he had a sudden realization. What he was hearing was not giggling but high-pitched sobs. The choked crying of a little girl.

John got out of bed. He paced cautiously toward the window and said, "Are you okay?"

The crying stopped.

John cupped his hands around his eyes and pressed his face against the windowpane to peer into the backyard. He saw no one.

Chapter Six

The window repairman was a wiry fellow in a paint-spattered overall. He was half bald, with hollow cheeks and sagging skin under his eyes. John Ferris was in the kitchen pouring himself a cup of home-brewed coffee when the doorbell rang. He brought his steaming mug to the door. When he opened it, the repairman looked at the coffee mug and shot John an unmasked look of annoyance, as if he'd been made to wait for hours.

The man said, "I'm here about a window."

"Great. It's in the back of the house," John said, trying to strike an agreeable tone.

"Is it a double-hung?" the man asked.

"I'm sorry?"

The repairman frowned. "The broken window. Is it a double-hung?"

"Uh . . . It's got two panes. The lower pane slides upward to open." John gestured with his hands as if he were opening a window.

"That's what double-hung means. Which pane is broken, top or bottom?"

"The bottom one. Here, let me show you." With coffee in hand, John stepped out the front door and onto the dry lawn, leading the repairman to the back of the house. As he walked, John took a sip of coffee. It tasted awful. He turned and spat it out on the lawn.

The repairman chuckled. "That good, huh?"

John ignored the man's comment and resumed his march. When he reached the broken window to the downstairs bedroom, John pointed at it in a see-I-told-you-so way.

The repairman pulled a narrow putty knife from the bottom pocket of his overall and scraped the strip of window seal in a way John found to be superfluous. He asked John, "Is that cardboard and duct tape you got there?"

"It keeps the wind out," John said trying not to sound defensive.

The repairman shook his head and tried to open the window. It didn't budge.

"The latch is shut," John said. "Do you want me to go around and open it?"

The man twisted his mouth and looked at John with drooping eyes. "That would be nice."

"Give me half a minute," John said and walked away. When he rounded the corner of the house, he muttered, "That would be nice. Jerk!" John dumped the rest of the coffee on the lawn and hurried into the house.

When he got to the bedroom, John was surprised to see the window was already open. "How'd you do that?" he asked.

The repairman held up the putty knife. "The latches on these old windows are crap," he said. "Here's a word to the wise. If you want to avoid break-ins, stick a shim under the latch."

"A shim?" John repeated.

The repairman rolled his eyes. "A little wedge made out of wood." He reached into his pockets and pulled something out. "Here. Take this one. It's on the house."

"Thanks," John said. He looked at the shim and said, "Do you need me to stick around? I need to get to the office."

The repairman shrugged. "The work order says I need to send the invoice to the property manager. It doesn't make one bit of difference to me if you stay or leave."

"Okay then," John said. He gathered his briefcase, his suit jacket, keys and wallet and left without saying another word.

Brenda Collins was already in the conference room, her long fingernails clacking away on an adding machine when John entered the room, bid her good morning, and took a seat. Brenda nodded, returned the greeting, and kept working.

Hardly an hour passed when she caught John rubbing his eyes and yawning. She said, "Looks like you had a rough night."

John avoided her gaze. "I stayed up late to watch a basketball game," he lied.

"I didn't know they play basketball at night."

"It was a taped game."

"I see," Brenda responded. "You're a big basketball fan?"

"Oh, yeah. I have season tickets to the Bulls," John said.

Brenda didn't seem to buy John's story. A moment later, she smiled. "I'm buying lunch today. Do you like fried chicken sandwiches?"

"Who doesn't like fried chicken sandwiches?" John answered.

"Good, because the place I'm taking you has the best in the world."

A couple of hours later, Brenda and John were sitting in a corner booth of Ruth's Famous Chicken. Brenda took it upon herself to order for the two of them. John slumped back in his seat and gazed out of the diner's window with an absent look.

"Are you okay?" Brenda asked.

John smiled. "I'm fine."

"How are things with your neighbors?"

"Splendid," John said. When Brenda frowned and cocked her head to the side, he added, "My wife thinks I should let bygones be bygones. She recommended I keep to myself and forget the whole deal."

"I see."

Seeing Brenda's skeptical expression, John said, "Katie is less confrontational than I am."

Brenda responded, "I mean, that's good advice if you live in a big city like Chicago. But you're in Maple Park. Around here, if someone buys a new TV set, everybody talks about it at the coffee shop for weeks. Word gets around. Do you know what I mean? And these people are your next-door neighbors. It'll be mighty hard to steer a wide berth around them."

"Believe me. There's nothing I'd rather do than go next door and give Ted Noland a piece of my mind."

Brenda shook her head. "You're going about it the wrong way. Haven't you ever heard the saying: you catch more bees with honey than with vinegar?"

"I don't want to catch bees."

"You're out in the country, John. We have a way of dealing with things."

John angled his head and said, "What do you suggest I do?"

Brenda puckered her lips and looked up at the ceiling, deep in thought. "I know. Why don't you invite them over for dinner?"

John scoffed. "Have you gone out of your mind?"

"Breaking bread together is the quickest way to smooth over disagreements. Every culture has done it for millennia," Brenda said.

John's eyelids fluttered. "There are two problems with your plan. Number one, I don't think I can tolerate eating an entire meal with the Noland clan."

"You'll have to suck it up," Brenda said.

"Number two, I can't cook. I can't very well invite people over for frozen pizza, can I?"

Brenda laughed. She rested her hands on the table and said, "You don't have to cook. Order pickup. There's an Italian kitchen a block away from the office. They prepare great lasagna trays. Just pick one up, reheat it in your oven for a few minutes, and you have yourself a gourmet meal. Everyone loves lasagna, even kids."

John considered her suggestion. As hard as he tried, he couldn't come up with a counterargument. He leaned forward in his seat and said, "Brenda, you're a genius."

"Come on. It doesn't take a rocket scientist to suggest picking up food."

"No, no, the last part you said. Even kids love lasagna. I still haven't seen their daughter, Sarah. If I invite them over, I'll finally get to meet her."

Brenda scrunched up her brow. "Yesterday, you told me you weren't very fond of kids."

"I'm not. But isn't it odd that no one's seen this little girl in ages? Why does she prowl the neighborhood at night, creating mischief?

Brenda scowled at him. "You want to bring them into your house so you can scold her for breaking your window."

"Not at all. But maybe, if I meet her face-to-face, I can convince the little brat to stop with her late-night visits."

"Wait a minute. Did she come back again last night?"

John leaned back in the booth, crossed his arms, and ignored her question. "Lasagna, a little garlic bread, maybe a bottle of wine. Tomorrow night. It's going to be great."

***

That evening, John entered the convenience store in Maple Park feeling light on his feet. He was a man with a purpose now.

Emily looked up from behind the counter and flashed him a broad smile. "You're becoming a regular," she said.

"Hello, Emily. How's my favorite cashier doing?"

"Every day is a miracle."

From the sparkle in her eye, John could tell she really meant it. The young lady was a ray of sunshine in this gray little town.

John approached the counter and said, "I wonder if you can give me a little advice. I want to bring a little care package to my neighbors, the Nolands. You mentioned they shop here. Would you happen to know what items they like?"

"Of course. Ted is a potato chips guy. He always buys a large bag. Mary-Beth has a bit of a sweet tooth. She loves those Ferrero Rocher chocolate bonbons. And they always pick up a bag of jellybeans for little Sarah."

"Perfect! You've been incredibly helpful." John gathered the items and returned to the cash register to check out. As Emily rang him up, he asked her, "How come your coffee here is so good, and the one I made at home this morning tasted like old motor oil?"

Emily laughed. "It's probably the water."

"The water?"

"The water in Maple Park is notoriously hard, full of minerals. Have you checked the salt level in your water softener?"

"Emily, don't get technical with me. I normally live in a high-rise with a concierge and a maintenance crew. My idea of major home repairs is changing a light bulb."

Emily said, "Your water softener is in the garage. It has a big plastic tank shaped like a cylinder that's supposed to be filled with salt pellets. Like those." Emily pointed to a pile of large plastic bags stacked in a corner. "If your house hasn't been lived in for a while, chances are the tank is empty, and that makes the water taste bad."

"I better buy a bag of salt pellets, then," John said.

Emily squeezed her lips together. "You better take two."

Emily was right. The water softener tank had no salt in it. The bottom held a few inches of standing water that emitted a smell approaching that of burnt plastic. The two 40-pound bags of salt pellets John purchased filled the tank two-thirds of the way. John's eyes and nose stung as the salt rattled into the tank and filled the air with a fine salty mist.

After emptying the second bag, John coughed, wiped his palms on the back of his pants, and headed into the house. He washed his hands, brushed his teeth, combed his hair, and headed for the Noland household to deliver the goodies he had just purchased and invite them to dinner the following night.

John felt like an intruder walking up the Nolands' walkway. At one point, he began to doubt Brenda's strategy. He considered turning around and returning home but forced himself to trudge on.

He took a deep breath when he reached the front door stoop and pressed the doorbell. He could hear the chime echo indoors. It had an old-fashioned feel of two-toned tubular bells, which resonated long after John's finger left the button.

John stepped back off the stoop, cleared his throat, and folded his hands together, the bag bearing the gifts swinging down by his knees. He glanced at the two picture windows on either side of the front door. The curtains were drawn.

The front door opened. Ted's body filled the crack of the opening. He looked stunned to see John.

"Hello, Ted," John said in as friendly a voice he could muster.

"Oh, he-hello, John," Ted stuttered. He stepped onto the outside landing and shut the door behind him. Ted wrinkled his brow. He looked nervous. John couldn't blame him after the events of the last couple of days. "What can I do for you?"

"I was at the convenience store, and I thought I'd pick up a few items for you and the family." John reached out and handed the bag to Ted, maintaining a distance between them.

Ted collected the bag, opened it, and looked inside. The puzzled look on his face lingered. He looked up and said, "John, this was very thoughtful of you. Thank you very much."

John shrugged and shook his head. "It's nothing. I wanted to apologize. I know we've gotten off to a bit of a rough start."

"No. I don't think so," Ted said. "Not at all."

John looked down and smiled with a slouch on his shoulders. "Yes, we have, Ted. I wanted to apologize to Mary-Beth in particular. I didn't mean to upset her the other day."

"John, please, don't give it another thought."

John studied Ted's expression. The puzzled look was gone. His neighbor's default homely smile had taken its place. "How is Mary-Beth?"

"She's terrific," Ted said, his smile now broadening, bearing the tips of his teeth.

"And Sarah?" Ted maintained his grin, but there was a subtle change in the shape of his eyes.

"Swell. Thanks for asking."

"I'm glad to hear it," John said. He wiped his palms together. "What I really came here for, Ted, is I want to invite you over to dinner tomorrow night. All of you." John wanted to be as specific as possible. "You, Mary-Beth, and Sarah."

The smile on Ted's face was becoming strained. He looked befuddled again. Ted's eyes blinked a couple of times before he replied, "Gee, John, that's mighty nice of you, but we wouldn't want to put you out."

"Not at all. It'll be my pleasure."

Ted chuckled nervously. "I-I don't know what to say."

John had clearly caught his neighbor off guard. "Then say yes. I'll see you around seven."

Ted nodded slowly. He straightened his neck, and his apprehension vanished. "Of course. Seven o'clock tomorrow. Mary-Beth and Sarah will be thrilled."

John backed away slowly and said, "See you tomorrow night, then."

"See you tomorrow, John. And thanks for the goodies."

John turned and walked home feeling satisfied.

See? That wasn't so bad.

Chapter Seven

Every day this week, Brenda had arrived at work before John. Today, when John walked into the conference room they used as their office, she wasn't there. John emitted a grunt of surprise and checked his wristwatch. It was past 9 AM. This was not like her.

He settled into his office chair, opened the file he had been working on the previous day, and got down to work. Thirty minutes passed, and Brenda still hadn't arrived. John began to worry that something was wrong. He pushed back in his chair, walked out of the conference room, and approached a receptionist.

"Excuse me, would you happen to know where Ms. Collins is?" John asked her.

"I'm sorry, Mr. Ferris," the receptionist said. "I was just about to inform you. Ms. Collins called in sick today."

"Nothing serious, I hope."

"Not at all. She has pink eye. She sends her apologies and says she'll try to be back in the office tomorrow."

John felt a sense of relief, even if her absence would slow down their progress. He thanked the receptionist and was about to walk away when the receptionist said, "She wanted me to tell you that she placed the order for the lasagna for you. And she asked me to remind you to pick it up before you leave for the day."

John smiled. "She thinks of everything, doesn't she?"

John returned to the conference room and buried himself in work. To make extra headway, he lunched on potato chips and coffee while entering figures in his computer's accounting software. By 5 p.m., his head was spinning.

A knock on the conference room door made him turn in his seat. It was the receptionist. "Mr. Ferris, I'm leaving for the day unless you need anything."

"Not at all, thank you," John said.

"You should go home too, sir. Your tray of lasagna is ready for pick up."

John checked the time and jumped to his feet. "Right. Thank you very much."

The aluminum tub of lasagna was large enough to feed a regiment of hungry soldiers. John figured that unless the Nolands ate like wolves, he'd have leftovers for several days.

John rushed home. He wanted to shower and tidy the house a little before the arrival of his neighbors. When he made the turn into his street, he was forced to slow his car to a stop. A group of children was playing an impromptu game of hockey in the middle of the road. They interrupted their match and moved out of the way to let John's car pass, waving at him as he drove by.

John waved back, unperturbed, marveling at how calm he was. Perhaps, dealing with kids wasn't as big a deal as he thought. Brenda's plan seemed to be already working. Sarah, the neighbor's daughter, hadn't come to bother him the night before. By the time he reached his front door, John Ferris felt so confident about the success of his little dinner party that he couldn't stop himself from whistling a tune.

The hot shower was soothing and invigorating. He toweled off, dressed in comfortable but stylishly casual slacks and a polo shirt, and set the dinner table with dishes he found in a kitchen cupboard.

He turned on the stereo and set the radio dial to a station that played cool jazz, adjusting the volume until it was just right. It was nearing 7 p.m. His neighbors would be there any minute. A tinge of anxiety washed over him.

The uneasiness grew as he wondered what he would talk to them about. He knew nothing about them, didn't have a glimmer of a notion of what their interests might be. He should have thought about this ahead of time and planned a few topics of engaging but safe conversation. It was too late to do anything about it now. The best he could do was keep the dialogue light.

It was seven o'clock. John set the tray of lasagna on the dinner table and removed the aluminum foil covering. It looked and smelled great. And John was starving. That bag of chips at lunchtime was far from satisfying. John opened a bottle of wine and placed it on the table but resisted the temptation to pour himself a glass. That would be rude.

Ten minutes passed by, and there was still no sign of the Nolands. How could they be so late? John wondered. They live next door.

At 7:20, as John's stomach began to growl, the doorbell rang. John breathed a sigh of relief. A minute longer, and he'd have started to eat without them.

He walked to the door, straightened his spine, and smiled broadly before opening it. He was preparing to welcome the Nolands into his home when he saw there was only one Noland on his front step—it was Ted, grinning sheepishly.

"Good evening," John said, looking around for Mary-Beth and little Sarah.

"Good evening, John," Ted said, "how are you?"

John expected Ted to apologize for his lateness and reassure him that his wife and daughter would be over momentarily. "I'm fine," John said, trying his best to be polite. "Nice to see you, neighbor."

Ted chortled. "Nice to see you too. I'm afraid I come as the bearer of bad news. You see, regrettably, we won't be able to have dinner with you tonight."

Ted avoided making eye contact with John. He looked nervous, downright anxious. John was finding it hard to maintain a courteous demeanor.

"The food is already on the table," John said.

"I apologize," Ted said, looking sincerely mortified. "You see, Sarah's not feeling well."

"I'm sorry to hear that. Nothing serious, I hope."

Ted chuckled nervously. "Oh, no. A simple strep throat. But she's—you know—contagious."

John frowned. He was genuinely disappointed. He had been looking forward to the two of them reaching an understanding of sorts with regard to the late-night visits. "My associate called in sick too today," John said to defuse the tension with a bit of small talk.

"Is that right?" Ted said with exaggerated interest.

"Pink eye," John said.

"That'll do it," Ted said. "Contagious as the dickens, pink eye is. Good thing she didn't come to work. That can wreak havoc in a busy office. The best one can do in these situations is stay home, don't you agree?"

John nodded. "I guess so."

Ted took a step backward. "Well, I best be going. I best check on Sarah before heading out to the pharmacy to pick up her prescriptions."

"Tell her I hope she feels better," John said.

"Sure thing, neighbor." Ted seemed to be hurrying away now.

"And Ted," John called out, "maybe we can do this another time."

"Yes, of course. Some other time."

John looked on as Ted walked nimbly down the sidewalk, entered his house, and quickly closed the door behind him. "I guess I'm having dinner alone," he said as he stepped into the house and shut the door.

He went to the dining table, poured himself a glass of wine, and scooped a generous portion of lasagna into a dish. John sat down and started eating. As he took a sip of wine, he told himself he could look forward to a quiet night. With Sarah being sick, there was no way she'd come to pester him. He could use a good night's sleep. Heck, he deserved it.

After dinner, he cleaned up the dining room, brushed his teeth, and phoned Katie to wish her a good night. She sounded as exhausted too. When he hung up the phone, he imagined how much more hectic their lives would be if they had children. He shuddered at the thought and slipped into bed.

He had barely turned the lights out when he slipped into a blissful sleep. By 10 p.m., he was so deeply asleep that it took a few seconds for John to realize someone was pounding on the newly replaced windowpane. The sound finally jolted him awake. His ears perked as the noise stopped. Then he heard the eerie sound of a little girl giggling. It gave him goosebumps. He lay in bed, trying to ignore the intrusion, hoping the noise would stop. It did for a moment. Then he heard a voice speak so clearly, he could have sworn it had come from inside his bedroom.

It said, "Find me!"

John remained frozen in his bed, breathing heavily, his wide-open eyes now adapted to the darkness. He must have been mistaken. The voice had to have come from the backyard. He wondered what Sarah was doing outside when she was ill.

Let it go, he told himself. *Forget about the whole thing.*

There was a loud pounding at the front door now. It paused for a few seconds before starting up again. John shot out of bed, grabbed his robe off a chair, and put it on as he hurried to the front of the house.

He jerked the door open. There was no one there.

John stepped into the cool night air and scanned the sidewalk. It was deserted. His neighbors' house was dark, as was every house on the street.

John felt his temper flaring. One thing he couldn't tolerate was being made a fool of. Sarah wasn't sick. She wasn't contagious at all. Ted had lied to him. For what reason, John couldn't fathom, but these nightly intrusions had to stop. Immediately.

He had tried using honey. Now it was time for some vinegar. John stomped his way to the front door of the Noland house and rang the doorbell. He rang it three more times before the door opened.

Mary-Beth stood in the foyer looking as pale as ever. Her eyes were wild, and her mouth was open in an o. Before she could utter a word, John said, "Where is she? I want to talk to her right now."

"What?" Mary-Beth said.

"Sarah. Go get her. And don't tell me she's sick. She was banging on my door with the strength of a bull."

Mary-Beth shook her head and, in a plaintive voice, said, "What do you want from us?"

"How about a little peace and quiet? Is that too much to ask?"

Mary-Beth flashed her teeth as she shouted, "Leave us alone!" and slammed the door in John's face.

John remained on the Nolands' doorstep for nearly a minute. Feeling utterly defeated, he finally turned and made his way back home. He lay in bed awake all night, considering what he'd have to do the next day.

***

What had started as a mere annoyance for John Ferris was evolving into something much darker and weighty. The events of the last few days and nights were beyond peculiar—they were alarming. The behavior of Ted and Mary-Beth Noland had crossed the bounds of eccentricity and entered the realm of shocking absurdity.

This matter was no longer an issue of John's aversion to the company of children. From what he had witnessed, John began to believe that Sarah's welfare was in jeopardy. What kind of parent allows their children to run around outside at night?

The longer John thought about it, the more confident he became that Ted and Mary-Beth were, at a minimum, neglectful and quite possibly abusive parents. And the basis for this was clear: Ted and Mary-Beth were certifiably insane.

It was an issue he could not ignore. Any way he looked at it, John Ferris reached the same conclusion. He had a moral obligation to act. But how?

He couldn't very well call the sheriff and tell him he thought the Nolands were crazy. Not after he had already dispatched him for the petty matter of a broken window. In his mind, John could hear the sheriff's voice reminding him that country folk had a different way of dealing with problems than city slickers. The law in this town was more likely to side with the Nolands than with an outsider like John.

What he needed was proof or at least solid evidence of neglect. What kind of evidence? John thought about it for the better part of the night, as he lay awake in bed. Gradually, a plan materialized in his head.

Brenda missed work again the next day. It was Friday and seeing as her eyes were still red and goopy, it made sense for her to take a long weekend and return Monday morning fully recovered rather than exposing the rest of the staff to an infectious disease. A part of John was relieved she wasn't there. She would have asked him how dinner with the Nolands had gone, and he'd have to tell her it was an unmitigated disaster. Worse, he knew he'd go on to disclose the plan he had hatched. A plan that, he suspected, she would strongly oppose.

John didn't have the time or energy to explain himself. He feared that in making the argument in defense of his strategy, he'd reveal things about his past Brenda Collins had no business knowing, issues he had never broached even with his wife. Yes, it was a relief she hadn't come to work.

John buried himself in his work for the entire workday. It was only on the drive home that he reviewed his plan for that night.

Chapter Eight

Early that morning, John called his old college roommate, Steve, who happened to be an avid amateur photographer. After a brief catching-up session, John got down to brass tacks.

"Steve, what's the best way to get a photograph in the dark?" John asked.

"Turn on a light," Steve replied in a deadpan voice.

"I want to take an outdoor picture. There are no lights to turn on."

"Then use a flash."

Steve didn't understand John's dilemma. He had to make himself clear.

"I can't have any light source. I have to take the picture in the dark."

There was a moment of silence from the other end of the line. "What exactly are you trying to do?"

John made up a story about a nighttime intruder tipping over his trash bin in the middle of the night.

"It's probably a raccoon," Steve said. "Just place a heavy brick on the lid of your bin."

"I want to take a picture to show the property manager so he can send the pest control service," John lied.

Steve seemed to be thinking about it. "You need two things: an infrared camera and an infrared light source."

"Sounds expensive," John said.

"Not at all. You can turn just about any conventional digital camera into an infrared one by removing a little filter from in front of the sensor."

John said, "I'm not very technically oriented."

"Piece of cake," Steve said. "You remove the backplate of the camera, carefully lift the screen, and you'll see the sensor smack in the middle of the camera box. Gently pry it up, and underneath you'll find a reddish filter. Just take it out, screw everything back together, and voila, you have an infrared camera. If you're having trouble, just watch a YouTube video. The entire process takes ten minutes tops."

"You mentioned something about an infrared light source," John said as he scribbled notes on a pad.

"Do this. Go to a pawn shop. Buy yourself an old digital camera. You can get one dirt cheap. And tell the guy you need a battery-powered infrared light source. They sell them as part of video surveillance systems. A decent one will cost you thirty bucks. Another thirty for an old camera, and you've got yourself a night surveillance system for well under a hundred bucks."

"Got it," John said. He thanked Steve profusely.

Before hanging up, Steve cautioned, "Just don't get yourself in trouble, John."

The manager at the pawnshop understood John's needs to a tee. For an extra twenty dollars, he popped the back of the camera open and removed the infrared filter himself. "You're all set to go," the manager said as he placed the two items in a plastic shopping bag. And then, to John's chagrin, he repeated Steve's admonishment, "Just don't get yourself in trouble now, you hear?"

At 9:45 p.m., John put on a black long-sleeve shirt, the darkest color trousers he could find, and a black Chicago Bulls baseball cap, with the bill flipped to the back. He considered darkening his skin with face paint, but he didn't have any, and the measure sounded a bit too extreme.

He grabbed his ersatz infrared camera and the invisible light source and stepped out into the chilly night.

John thought it would be best to take some practice pictures to ensure the camera worked as Steve had said it would. He activated the light source in his left hand and pointed it to a dark spot up in the vacant lot across from his house. With the camera in his dominant hand, he snapped a photograph.

When he checked the camera's screen, he was amazed. Details he couldn't see with the naked eye appeared in a grayish-green tinge. With a surge of confidence, he positioned himself in the space between his house and the Nolands' and waited.

To pass the time, he panned the camera across his backyard and snapped several photos. He waited some more. He glanced at the Nolands' house to check for activity. Quite innocently, he pointed the infrared light source and the camera in the direction of his neighbors' house.

Immediately, floodlights hanging from the eves of the Noland house turned on, illuminating John in a blinding glare. The front door of his neighbors' house whipped open and out stepped Mary-Beth in a night robe.

"What the hell are you doing? You pervert!" Mary-Beth screamed. John lowered his equipment and tried to hide it behind his back. "What are you hiding there?" Mary-Beth asked. "Is that a camera?" She turned toward the entrance of her home and shouted, "Ted, he's got a freaking camera!"

"Look," John said, "I can explain."

As John took a step toward her, Mary-Beth leaped back. She grabbed the handle of the front door and said, "Explain it to the police," before slamming it shut.

The floodlights turned off. John stood in the darkness for a moment before shuffling back inside his house.

"Great. Just great," John muttered to himself. He finally understood what Steve and the pawnshop manager meant when they warned him not to get into trouble. At least, he hadn't painted his face black. He decided to change into clothes that didn't arouse as much suspicion and opted for pajamas. He had hardly changed when his doorbell rang.

He went to the front foyer and, after taking a deep breath, opened the door.

A man in a tan uniform stood on the outside stoop. He flashed John a look of disdain and said, "I'm deputy Frank Billing with the Sheriff's Department. We got a call about a peeping Tom."

John wrinkled his forehead. "Peeping Tom? No, there's been a huge misunderstanding."

"So, you deny hiding outside taking pictures of your neighbor's house?" the deputy asked.

"I—I didn't take pictures of their house."

"Do you own surveillance equipment?"

"Just a camera. A lousy digital camera. I didn't take pictures of their house. I can show you if you'd like."

The deputy hooked his thumbs on his belt. "I'm sure you've deleted them by now."

"I didn't delete a darn thing. I didn't take pictures of their house!" John shouted.

"Sir, I'm going to have to ask you to bring the volume of your voice down a notch, do you understand? You better calm the hell down, or you'll find yourself in a world of pain."

John raised his palms and lowered his voice. "I'm calm. I'm calm."

The deputy said, "Are you familiar with the federal statute on stalking?"

John slowly shook his head and said, "No. Why would I be?"

"I understand you're not from around these parts. Well, let me make something clear. We have a zero-tolerance policy in our county when it comes to stalking and voyeurism."

"As you should. I was doing neither."

"You're lucky your neighbors are decent, understanding folk. Kindhearted to a fault if you ask me. Mr. Noland declined to press charges. He opted to have me give you a warning. But just so you know, we've got our eyes on you. If you harass them again in any way, I'll make it a point to take you in custody personally." The deputy lifted his thick index finger and poked John in the chest. With a grimace, he said, "You watch yourself, mister."

The officer turned on his heels and walked away to his patrol car. John entered his home, shut the door, and cursed under his breath.

He walked back to his bedroom and wondered if he should delete the photographs he had taken in case things escalated. John picked up his camera and turned it on. He began deleting the pictures, one by one until he came to one that stopped him cold.

It was a photograph of his backyard. In the center of the frame was a strange oval glow of light. John peered at it and couldn't make out what it was. Something made him decide not to delete it.

Chapter Nine

John was in the kitchen the following morning, tying his necktie as the coffee machine gurgled. He hadn't told his wife about the incident with the Nolands involving the infrared camera. Not only was he embarrassed, but he also figured there was no point in worrying her. He would behave. From now on, he'd stay away from his neighbors and ignore little Sarah's taunting.

What had she said the other night? *Find me!*

Not a chance, little girl.

John Ferris had no time for fun and games. If the Nolands were okay with their daughter running amok in the neighborhood at night, it was fine with him too. He'd just stop at the drug store and buy himself a good pair of silicone earplugs so he wouldn't have to hear her annoying giggling.

As he poured himself a mug of coffee (which tasted much better since adding salt pellets to the water softener), the doorbell rang.

John wondered who it could be at this early hour as he walked the hallway to the front foyer. He opened the door to see the massive frame of Sheriff Brad Thornsby. The law enforcement official had a worried look on his face.

He asked John, "Going to work on a Saturday morning?"

"I thought I'd best limit my presence in the neighborhood," John replied.

"Mighty fine idea," the sheriff said. "Mind if I come in?"

John showed the officer in and offered him a cup of coffee, which the sheriff politely declined. The two men sat down across each other at the kitchen table.

Sheriff Thornsby clasped his hands together over the kitchen table, groaned, and said, "Mr. Ferris, I wanted to get your version of the events of last night."

John took a sip of coffee and said, "There's not much to say. I happened to be outside, and Mrs. Noland got the wrong idea."

"Please illuminate me. What exactly were you doing outside at night?"

John put his mug down and said, "That little girl of theirs has been coming over almost every night, at ten o'clock on the nose. Maybe it's none of my business, but what kind of parent lets their little kids run around after dark?"

Sheriff Thornsby gave John a stern look. "I know you've made that assertion the last time we spoke. But the Nolands are adamant their child could not possibly be out last night."

"You think I'm making this up," John said.

"Now, I didn't say that."

"Why would I make it up?"

"Beats me."

"You gotta admit, the Nolands are an odd couple," John said.

The sheriff looked down at his hands and said, "I'll admit they're a little unconventional."

Sensing a slight shift in momentum, John pushed on. "I mean, their little girl, Sarah . . . it looks like no one's seen her in years. Not my landlord, not the clerk at the convenience store, not even you. Doesn't she have any friends? Does she go to school?"

The sheriff leaned back in his chair and locked eyes with John. "I thought she was a nuisance to you. Now, you're acting like you're concerned about her welfare. So, which is it?"

"Both," John said. "You're the sheriff in this town. Aren't *you* worried?"

The sheriff crossed his arms. "I'll tell you what, Mr. Ferris. I'll go check on the little Noland girl right now. You go ahead and clear out of here and get yourself to work. And try to keep a low profile for the rest of your stay in Maple Park."

"Will you call me?" John requested. "I want to know she's all right."

The sheriff puckered his mouth. It took him a moment to think about it. "Sure. I'll call you after I check in on them."

The sheriff reached across the table, and the two men shook hands.

John Ferris had barely arrived at the office when Sheriff Thornsby called him on the phone.

"I have good news for you, Mr. Ferris," the sheriff said.

"You saw Sarah."

"I did not. But the Nolands are prepared to put the incident behind them and agreed not to press charges against you."

"That's what your deputy told me last night." John was puzzled. "Did I hear you right? You did not see their daughter?"

"She's not here. Ted Noland told me Sarah's been staying at her grandmother's house in Peoria since Thanksgiving Day."

John almost dropped the phone. "That's not possible. I got here after Thanksgiving. And you saw the broken window with your own eyes. Sarah did that."

"The Nolands dispute that. They said she couldn't possibly have done that."

John shook his head. "The day I arrived in Maple Park, they brought her over to greet me."

Now the sheriff sounded perplexed. "I thought you said you never met her."

"I didn't. I mean, she was there, but I didn't see her. And when I invited them to my house for dinner, Ted didn't mention anything about his daughter visiting her grandmother."

The sheriff was even more mystified by this. "You invited the Nolands for dinner?"

"They didn't show up," John said. "I mean, they canceled on account that Sarah was ill." John could hear the sheriff groan. John added, "Maybe they're hiding her."

"That's not the case," the sheriff said more decisively. "I asked them if I could take a look in their house. They could have refused, but they didn't. I checked every room. The girl isn't here, and the house is in order. In fact, the entire home is immaculate, including Sarah's room."

John remained unconvinced. "How can Sarah be at her grandmother's house when school is back in session?"

"She's homeschooled," the sheriff said.

"I'm telling you, sheriff. They're hiding something. That girl is in my backyard at 10 p.m. every night like clockwork. I don't know where they're keeping her, but she's sure as heck not in Peoria."

"I'll tell you what I'll do for you, Mr. Ferris. And understand that I'm going way beyond what protocol mandates for these situations. I'm going to have a deputy stake out your neighborhood tonight. You say she comes at ten o'clock sharp? My man will be there to spot her."

John exhaled. "That won't work. If he's sitting in his patrol car, he'll stick out like a sore thumb."

"I'll have him use an unmarked vehicle and instruct him to wear plains clothes. Sound good?"

A troubling thought flitted through John's mind. "Can you tell me the name of the deputy you'll dispatch?"

"Frank Billing. I believe the two of you met last night," the sheriff said.

John rolled his eyes. "Oh, great."

"Mr. Ferris, please understand we're a small department. We have a limited staff. It's either deputy Billing or nothing. Do you have a flashlight?"

John thought about it. "The one on my cell phone," he replied.

"That'll do. If you see or hear something tonight, flash your cell phone out your front door. That will be the signal. Deputy Billing will take care of the rest."

John struggled to maintain his focus on his work that day. He kept thinking about Ted Noland's claim that Sarah had been away at her grandmother's house this entire time. What a bald-faced lie! If that wasn't enough to irk him, the prospect of coming face-to-face with deputy Frank Billing created even more anxiety.

The only consolation was that Sheriff Brad Thornsby sounded sincere and competent even if he was skeptical of John's story. Who could blame him for his doubts? The whole chain of events was hard to believe. When he left the office to get lunch, John started to doubt himself too.

Chapter Ten

John Ferris rarely drank coffee in the evening; the caffeine disrupted his already erratic sleep schedule. But tonight, he needed to stay alert, so he brewed a pot after finishing up his dinner. Around 9 p.m., he washed his dishes and cleaned up the kitchen, standing barefoot on the cold tile floor. As he dried his hands on a small towel, he looked down at his feet and decided he better put a pair of sneakers on if there was going to be any excitement tonight.

At 9:45, he positioned a chair to the side of his bedroom window behind the curtains, just out of view, and sat fully alert for his stakeout. The ring of his cell phone startled him.

"Hello?" John said.

"This is Frank Billing from the sheriff's department."

The deputy sounded annoyed.

"Good evening, deputy," John said.

"I just wanted to let you know I'm parked outside your house."

"Thank you, deputy. I appreciate it."

"I have no intention of wasting too much of my time, do you understand? At 10:15 sharp, I'm out of here. You got that?"

The man was a never-ending source of delight.

"Got it," John said.

"You remember what it is you have to do? In case you're feeling threatened by a little girl?" Sarcasm was dripping from every word the deputy spoke.

John frowned. "I'll shine a flashlight out my front door."

"Attaboy!" the deputy said in a condescending tone. "Ten fifteen rolls around, don't even bother with that flashlight. I'll be gone."

The deputy hung up. John looked at the phone and quietly cursed. It didn't matter what the deputy thought. In a few minutes, John would be vindicated. He had a gut feeling that little Sarah would be coming out to play tonight. As he thought about it, the hair on his arms stood on end.

Ten minutes passed. The house was so quiet that the only things John could hear were the pulsing of his blood through his ears and the sound of his breathing.

He checked the time. It was 9:59. John heard the now familiar sound of a girl giggling. He angled his head by the edge of the window and tried looking outside. He saw nothing.

There was another giggle, louder now, and a voice. "Find me."

He jumped out of his chair and looked out the window. The backyard was empty.

He heard the voice again. "Find me!"

The words penetrated his ear canals, crystal clear. He realized they could not be coming from outside the house. That's when he heard the creaking of footsteps coming from upstairs.

Quietly, John made his way out of the bedroom. He paced up the hallway to the front door, which he noticed was unlocked. John opened the door, turned on his cell phone's flashlight, and waved the beam into the darkness. He heard a car door slamming shut and turned to keep an eye on the staircase.

John could not fathom what would compel a little girl to sneak into his house after dark, but the decision would be her downfall. The gig was up. The sheriff's deputy would see her with his own eyes, and the Nolands' denials would fall on deaf ears.

Deputy Billing stepped onto the front porch with a groan and said, "This better be good."

John placed his index finger on his lips. "Shhh," he whispered, "she's upstairs."

Frank Billing cocked an eyebrow and twisted his mouth in a show of doubt. He stepped in the door as quietly as his stiff shoes allowed and made his way up the stairway without uttering a word. John followed him close behind.

When he got to the top of the stairs, the deputy asked John, "Where's the light switch?"

John turned the light on for him. The deputy walked the hallway, looking unimpressed. He opened the first bedroom door, glanced inside, and proceeded to the next room. After looking in all the rooms, Frank Billing said, "There's no one here."

"We should check inside the closets," John said.

The deputy flashed him an exasperated look. "Do you want me to look under the beds too?"

"Sure. Why not?"

The deputy said, "I'm done with this farce." He started descending the stairs. He called out, "Next time you feel threatened by a little girl, hire yourself a private bodyguard." He stopped at the front door, faced John, and said, "Man, you need help," and tapped his fingers on his temple.

John looked on from the threshold of the front door as the sheriff's deputy got into his unmarked car and drove away. He stood there a moment thinking. He shut the door and decided that if Frank Billing wasn't going to comb the upstairs of his home, he would.

He spent over half an hour looking into every space that might conceal a little girl until he gave up and abandoned his search. John plodded back downstairs, drank a glass of water from the kitchen tap, and made his way to the bedroom.

He wasn't dreaming, and he wasn't crazy. He had heard Sarah's voice. A girl's voice anyway, a voice that sounded oddly familiar. He tried to replay it in his head as he brushed his teeth. Where had he heard that voice before? From the other night, when Sarah was in the backyard, of course. He spat in the sink and rinsed his mouth. No. He had heard it long before. He was sure of it. A long time ago.

He grabbed a towel to dry his hands and mouth and realized his face was wet with tears.

Chapter Eleven

It was a bright Sunday morning. John could hear the bells of a church ringing in the distance, the voice of a finch chirping from the bough of a live oak.

He considered getting dressed and driving to the office but quickly dismissed the idea. He confessed to himself that he'd only be doing it as an escape, to avoid facing more meaningful issues.

If he was going to push through with what he was planning to do, he had better fix himself a strong cup of coffee first. And get out of his pajamas. He couldn't hold a serious conversation, even over the phone, without the proper attire.

Thirty minutes later, he settled onto the sofa, held out his telephone, and dialed a number he hadn't dialed in who knows how long.

The raspy voice of a man answered after five dial tones. "Hello?"

John took a deep breath. "Hi, Dad."

"What happened?"

"What do you mean what happened?" John asked.

"You never call. I figured something must have happened." John's father didn't express an ounce of concern. He spoke matter-of-factly, as he always had.

"I just called to talk," John said. "Are you doing okay?"

"I can't complain," his father said. "I just got back from church. I'm about to head over to see your mom, bring her some fresh flowers."

John knew his father went to the cemetery every day, rain, or shine, but changed the flowers on his mother's grave only once a week.

"That's great, Dad," John said.

His dad said, "You should visit her more often. She's always asking about you."

John knew his father had long conversations with his dearly departed wife. But the stoic man had never admitted to his son that he heard her talking back. Perhaps, he was just getting old.

"I'm out of town for a while," John said. "Maybe, we can visit her together when I get back to Chicago."

"Sure. Why not," John's father said. "Now, are you going to tell me what the hell is bothering you?"

John didn't hesitate. If he was going to bring up the taboo subject of the Ferris family, the topic that had remained unspoken for so many years, he might as well do it without beating around the bush. "I want to talk about Jessica," John said. "I want you to tell me about my sister."

John could hear his father let out a forced exhalation. In a lower voice, he said, "I knew sooner or later you'd bring this up. To be honest, I'm surprised it took you so long to get around it."

"I have a right to know," John said.

"Sure, you do. Just do me a favor. Don't tell your mom that I told you."

***

As soon as Katie Ferris answered the phone, she was alarmed by her husband's tone. "John? Are you alright?"

"Katie, I had a sister. A twin sister. Her name was Jessica."

"What?" Katie said. "What are you talking about?"

"She died of leukemia when we were four years old."

It took Katie a few seconds to process what her husband had said. "How come you never told me about her?"

"My memory of her was so faint I wasn't sure she was real. Part of me believed I had made her up. You know, the way children sometimes have imaginary friends. I thought my mental picture of her was only a dream."

Katie sounded confused. "Didn't your parents talk to you about her?"

"Never. It was a taboo subject in our home. My mother wouldn't tolerate it. She made my father get rid of all her toys and dresses. It was such a painful subject for my mom that she pretended she never had a daughter. And my father went along so as not to upset her."

"Is there a reason you're telling me about this today?"

John said, "I talked to my father this morning. He told me everything. I think the old man was glad to get it off his chest."

Katie said, "Your father called you out of the blue to tell you about your twin sister?"

John rubbed his brow. "I called him. Something made me remember her."

There was a long pause. "John, you're worrying me."

"Katie, I hear her voice sometimes."

"Whose voice?"

"Jessica's. I know this sounds crazy. I think she talks to me."

Katie's voice came through gently, patiently. "John, you've been working so hard. I can't imagine the stress you've been under lately. Why don't you come home for a few days? I miss you."

"Do you think this is why children make me feel uneasy?" John asked his wife.

Katie took a long time to answer. "I think grief takes many forms. Everyone deals with the loss of their loved ones in different ways. Your mother dealt with the pain using denial. Perhaps, your ache was so great you couldn't bear the thought of it happening again, of having to relive the loss of a child. Maybe, that's why you never wanted to have children of your own. Look, John, the bond between twins is unique. It's unbreakable. Part of you died with Jessica, but part of her is still alive in you."

His wife's words rang true. John fought to contain the tempest of emotions swirling inside him. He said, "I have to go, Katie. I'll call you back later."

"Do you want me to drive over? I can make it there in a couple of hours."

"No need. I'm fine, really," John said. "There's just one more thing I need to tell you, Katie."

"What is it, John?"

"I love you," he said, feeling every syllable.

John hung up the phone and wept for the first time in his adult life.

Chapter Twelve

The digital camera lay on the bedside table. Something made John pick it up. He wanted to take a second look at that strange photograph with the glowing light. He pushed the power button, waited for the camera to boot up, and gasped. The photograph pulled up on the screen, but it had changed. It was as though the light had retracted, and now, an amorphous shape was barely visible behind it. Could it be the image of a small child?

John studied the picture and wondered if there was something particular about infrared photographs that made them change over time. He considered calling his friend, Steve to ask him but was afraid of what he'd say. He powered off the camera and put it back on the bedside table.

John got dressed in a hurry. More than ever, he couldn't shake the thought that the Nolands were hiding something. John had suspected them of being neglectful parents. Now he wondered if the truth were worse. What if they were abusing Sarah, and she was crying out to him for help? His conscience told him he had to act. Calling Sheriff Thornsby would be a waste of time, especially in light of the previous night's events with Deputy Frank Billing.

No. John would have to take matters into his own hands. He had to be smart about this. If he screwed up, the Nolands would undoubtedly press charges against him, and he'd be in a world of trouble.

John had to break into the Nolands' home while they're away. For all he knew, his neighbors were keeping Sarah locked up in their house, in an attic or a cellar Sheriff Thornsby failed to inspect. John had to see the inside of their home with his own two eyes.

But what if they returned unexpectedly? He'd be sunk. He better think about this some more. If the Nolands went for their routine excursion to the convenience store, they'd be back too soon. If he waited too long to act, he'd miss out on a great opportunity.

John decided to drive to the convenience store to see if he might spot the Nolands there. Of course. That would give him more information on their whereabouts.

He grabbed his keys, got into his car, and drove away. A few minutes later, he saw that the Nolands' car wasn't in the convenience store parking lot. John wasn't satisfied. He parked his car and went inside the store. He pretended to do some light shopping, picking up a loaf of wheat bread and a pack of chewing gum before going to the cash register, where Emily greeted him with a warm hello and a winning smile.

John had barely finished his hello when Emily said, "I just saw your neighbors, the Nolands."

"Oh, yeah?" John said.

"They always stop in on Sunday mornings on their way to Peoria," Emily said, ringing him up. "Mrs. Noland's mother lives out there. They go and check on her every week."

It was all John needed to hear. He slapped a five-dollar bill on the counter and grabbed his items before Emily had a chance to bag them. He was halfway to the door when she called out, "You forgot your change!"

"Keep the change," John shouted with a smile. She had certainly earned it.

If the Nolands were driving to Peoria, they'd be gone for hours. Now, it was only a matter of getting inside their home. He had a pretty good idea of how he would do it.

Chapter Thirteen

John sped home from the convenience store. He turned into the street of his home with a screeching of tires. When he saw a skateboard seemingly abandoned on the road ahead of him, he slammed his foot on the brake, the front of his car stopping less than a foot from the board. A red-headed boy with freckles, eleven or twelve years old by John's estimate, ran into the street and picked up the skateboard. He stopped in front of the car's grill to smile and wave at John.

John waved back at the kid with a sense of astonishment. When the boy reached the sidewalk, John sighed with relief. He better settle down, he thought. The last thing he needed was an accident.

John coasted to his home and turned off the car engine. The Nolands' car was not in their driveway. How could it be? They had gone to Peoria. It would be hours before they'd be back. John entered his home and prepared himself.

There was one item he needed. Would he be able to find it? He stepped into the garage where, between cardboard boxes, he found an old metal toolbox with a rusty latch. He opened it and looked inside. There were several mismatched screwdrivers, a few wrenches, some loose sockets, and on the very bottom, the specific object John was searching for: a putty knife.

Hadn't the man who replaced his broken windowpane used it to slip the latch of the double-hung window of his bedroom? Hadn't he said this was a common security issue among the homes in the neighborhood? John only hoped the Nolands had the same type of windows and that they hadn't secured them somehow.

John slipped the putty knife into the back pocket of his jeans. He opened the front door and looked outside. The last thing he needed was another neighbor to witness him breaking into a house. The police would be there in no time, and he'd have a lot of uncomfortable explaining to do.

Thankfully, the street was deserted. Even the boy with the skateboard had left. John stepped out and locked his front door behind him. He went up the path between his house and his neighbors' and hopped over a low fence to get into their backyard.

He walked past a large living room picture window and approached a double-hung window that seemed to lead to a downstairs bedroom. He took the putty knife out of his pant pocket and inserted the blade between the frames of the upper and lower panes. He jiggled the putty knife around but couldn't seem to move the latch. Perhaps, the operation was a lot harder than the window repairman had claimed. Or maybe this window's latch was just stuck.

He walked ten more feet to another window of the same kind. This time, when he slid the tool into position, he felt initial resistance followed by a smooth movement. With a surge of excitement, John placed the putty knife back in his pocket. He grasped the frame of the bottom pane with both hands and pushed up. The window slowly opened.

John took another furtive glance before entering the opened window headfirst. It was an awkward maneuver that ended with him doing a sort of summersault onto the floor. But he was in!

John got to his feet and looked around. The room was a study converted into a sewing room. John rubbed his nose and told himself he may as well get started. He opened a closet door and looked inside. A few winter coats were hanging from the rod, but nothing else.

"This room's clear," John said.

When he stepped out of the room into a hallway, John had the eerie feeling that he was not alone. He stopped and called out, "Hello? Is anyone here?" After a moment's hesitation, he said, "Sarah? If you're here, don't be scared. I won't hurt you." There was no reply.

He walked down the hallway, past an old-fashioned grandfather clock into the next room, the downstairs bedroom. John looked in the closet and under the bed. It was empty. He proceeded systematically through the entire downstairs of the home before trying a door off of the kitchen that stuck to the frame. He shoved it open with his shoulder. There were steps that led to a basement. John flipped a wall switch to turn on the lights and proceeded down the steps. The cellar had dank walls of red brick, crumbling in places, and smelled of mildew. From the hanging cobwebs, John got the impression that no one had been down there for a while. He saw the furnace in a corner, an old sofa stacked on end, a set of tires, and some gardening tools. He moved around the space methodically, checking behind boxes, and opening a discarded dresser, until he was satisfied Sarah wasn't there.

John went back to the kitchen and pulled the cellar door shut, just like he had found it.

It was time to go upstairs. As John climbed to the second floor, he couldn't help but notice that, except for the basement, the house was very tidy and well maintained. It even smelled fresh. The closer he got to the upstairs landing, the more he detected the aroma of flower-scented deodorizer sprayed with a heavy hand. He decided to follow the smell. It led him into a small bedroom, where something made him stop on the threshold.

A small bed, covered by a pink comforter featuring a Disney movie character, stood with its head against the far wall in the middle of the room. Dolls and small stuffed animals covered a wall shelf. A low table stacked with blocks and jars of silly putty was wedged in one corner of the room. Next to it, on the floor, was a toy piano. Bags of jellybeans, like the ones he had bought for her at the convenience store, spilled from a large wicker basket sitting on the carpet, pushed against the wall.

"Sarah?" John called out. He crossed the room and opened the closet door. Tiny dresses hung in an orderly arrangement. A shelf held folded pants, sweaters, and undergarments. A dozen pairs of small shoes stood on the floor with their toes lined up with the floorboard.

John closed the closet door and kneeled to look under the bed. He found a few storybooks but nothing else. He got back up, brushed his knees, and started walking out of the bedroom.

He stopped at the doorway and turned. There was something that didn't jibe. Sarah was nine years old. But the furnishings of the room and the toys seemed more appropriate for a much younger child. John certainly wasn't an expert on these matters, to be sure. But the size of the clothes left little doubt. If Sarah was nine, she was a runt.

He took a last look around him. For the first time, his attention focused on the wallpaper. It featured zoo animals, lions, giraffes, elephants, and monkeys. The drawings were very infantilized. Again, not what he would have expected in the bedroom of a spunky nine-year-old who snuck out after dark and threw rocks through windows. Compared to the rest of the house, the colors of the wallpaper appeared faded, and a flap had lifted at a poorly aligned seam.

John shook his head and walked up the hallway to the only other upstairs room. This had to be the master bedroom, where Ted and Mary-Beth slept. As he neared the door, John began to feel a little lightheaded. Getting down on his knees and getting up quickly was doing a number on him. He hadn't realized how out of shape he was and wondered if he should start going to the gym from time to time.

The dizziness got worse, and when he grasped the door handle to the Nolands' bedroom, his ears buzzed with a high-pitched ringing. John felt lightheaded. He brought his hand up to his forehead and leaned on the door handle, putting his entire weight on it. The door flew open, and John tumbled to the floor in a daze.

As he lay there, with the room spinning, he heard muffled voices but couldn't make out from where they were coming. The voices grew louder, echoing in his head. He felt a weight on his chest, making it hard to breathe. John's entire body grew heavy. He struggled to move his limbs, to focus his eyes.

The voices became louder now and clearer to the point he could distinguish two clear tones, a mid-range male pitch and the higher range of a woman's voice. The conversation between the two was heated. Shouting soon ensued.

At that point, something inexplicable happened. John was able to see a man and a woman standing in the bedroom, which had been unoccupied only seconds earlier. He knew immediately that he was witnessing a type of apparition. The bodies of the man and woman were poorly defined, almost translucent. They appeared more like suspended holograms than flesh and blood.

Nonetheless, John was able to recognize them. They were Ted and Mary-Beth Noland, or better yet, an essence of them, an imprint they might have left behind in the ether. If their specters had noticed John's presence, they made no sign of it. They kept on arguing.

Mary-Beth said, "I'm tired of living in this town, in this house. There's nothing to do. No good schools for Sarah."

Ted replied, "We've been over this a million times before. We have no money. Once I recover my business losses, we can talk about this again. In the meantime, I suggest you drop the subject."

"Drop the subject? All you've ever cared about was money."

Ted put his hands on his hips and leaned forward. "Of course, I care about money. Do you know what it costs to live in the city? Do you have any idea what the tuition of a private school runs?"

"I can get a job," Mary-Beth said.

Ted laughed scornfully. "No wife of mine is going to work. Who would hire you anyway? You have no skills. You're worthless. You'd be out on the street without if it weren't for me."

"I don't have to take this from you."

"Oh, yeah?" Ted said. "What are you going to do about it?"

"I'm going to leave you, Ted. I'm going to take Sarah and move in with my parents."

Ted gritted his teeth. "You will do no such thing." He grabbed Mary-Beth by the jaw and shoved her backward. Mary-Beth lost her footing and stumbled back. Just then, a little girl entered the room. Mary-Beth crashed into her. The girl was propelled against the bedroom door. The back of her little head struck the door handle hard.

For a few moments, all was quiet. Then, Mary-Beth said, "Sarah?"

The little girl was sprawled on the floor. She did not respond.

Mary-Beth's voice jumped a notch. "Sarah? Sarah! Oh my God, Sarah!"

Mary-Beth cradled her daughter's head in her lap and caressed her cheeks. The girl's eyes didn't open.

Mary-Beth shrieked, "What are you waiting for? Call an ambulance!"

A ghostly chime rang out, the gong of the downstairs grandfather clock. John rolled his body just enough to see the digital face of a bedside alarm clock. It read 10 p.m.

Ted knelt next to his wife and put his fingers on his lifeless daughter's neck. He murmured, "It's too late for an ambulance. She's dead."

As Mary-Beth let out a blood-curling scream, John Ferris jerked awake. He was in a cold sweat. He sat up on the floor, wondering how long he'd been out. Had he been unconscious? John wasn't sure. Everything he saw had the veneer of truth. Even now that he was awake, he couldn't brush away the vision as a bad dream.

Hours must have passed. He could tell from the position of the sun in the sky, which was well below its zenith. John rubbed his brow, trying to grasp the situation. Ted and Mary-Beth had killed their daughter. It was an accident, to be sure, but little Sarah was dead. Yet, they continued to pretend she was alive. Why?

John considered what his wife had told him over the phone. *Grief takes many forms. Everyone deals with the loss of their loved ones in different ways.*

He thought about how his parents had dealt with the loss of his sister, Jessica. His mother had tried to erase every trace of Jessica to avoid facing her pain. The Nolands had taken the opposite approach. They pretended Sarah was still alive. From what he could surmise, they hadn't told anyone about their daughter's death, hadn't alerted the authorities.

John began to wonder how they disposed of her body. As the thought crossed his mind, he heard the cry of a girl's voice. "Find me!"

The sound sent a shiver down John's spine. He slowly got to his feet. He was quite sure the sound had come from the girl's bedroom. He paced up the hallway and gazed into the room. It was empty. Still, something told him she was here.

He looked at the ceiling, then the carpeted floor, before his eyes scanned the four walls. They stopped on that flap of rolled-up wallpaper next to the mismatched crease.

With his eyes fixed on the lifted paper, John approached the wall. He grabbed the raised flap with both hands and pulled on it. The faded wallpaper peeled off the wall in a big sheet. John ripped it off and looked at the exposed drywall underneath. He could hardly believe his eyes.

Chapter Fourteen

The exposed wall had bands of dried spackle, roughly applied, in the shape of a rectangle, about three feet wide and five feet tall. It appeared a section of the wall had been removed, then reapplied and patched up by a nonprofessional.

John rapped on the wall with his knuckle, expecting a hollow sound but got quite the opposite. The knock had a dull, hard-packed tone.

John Ferris took a moment to consider what he was about to do. Was he really going to punch a hole in his neighbor's wall? There was no way the Nolands wouldn't notice when they returned home. John knew that this was a point of no return if he proceeded. And odds were very good he'd have to have an uncomfortable conversation with Sheriff Thornsby in the very near future.

He knew he was stalling. John had already crossed that point of no return when he broke into his neighbors' house. And as far as leaving evidence of his break-in, the torn wallpaper was more than sufficient. There was no point in stopping now. John had to see what was behind this wall. He had to confirm his suspicions.

More importantly, Sarah had called out to him. She was depending on him. He couldn't let her down.

John took the putty knife out of his pocket and scraped away the dry spackling compound from the left vertical band until he could see a narrow gap between sections of drywall. As he opened the space, he detected an unexpected smell . . . salt.

He was making little progress trying to whittle away the sheetrock with the corner of the putty knife and decided on a more pragmatic approach. John drove the blade of the putty knife into the wall with a good, strong thrust. The sharp edge of the tool formed a deep gash. The force of the blow drove the blade down to the handle.

John pulled it out and stabbed the wall again at a slightly different angle. This time, he managed to poke a hole in the wall. To his amazement, a familiar material began pouring out of the aperture. They were white oval pebbles that John immediately recognized as salt pellets used for water softeners.

What could water softener salt be doing inside the wall? He pulled on the edge of the damaged sheetrock with his fingers and managed to pull off a chunk of wall, about three inches squared. More white pellets fell out, but one remained in the hole, suspended somehow.

The smell of salt grew stronger now, but John noticed another strangely sweet aroma. He grasped the pellet that was somehow hovering in the wall's hole and noticed it was connected to a thin thread. He took a closer look and noticed it wasn't a thread at all; it was a light brown strand of hair.

John took his cell phone out of his pocket, turned on the flashlight app, and inspected the gap in the wall. He saw more hair joined together in a bundle. And beneath the lump of hair was some cloth: a faded yellow cotton fabric printed with tiny strawberries.

John grasped the hole's edges with both hands and pulled with all his might. A large section of the wall broke off, sending

John stumbling back a step. Salt pellets rattled to the floor like a cascade of ice cubes. What they revealed horrified John.

A small body stood in the wall, wedged between vertical wooden beams. Its skin was dry, ruffled and rigid, a swarthy color, like the flesh of a mummy, the mummy of a child. The mouth of the tiny corpse hung open. Her eyes were hollow spaces; her nose was pinched. She was wearing a short-sleeved summer dress—the same dress John witnessed in his preternatural vision. John pressed his fist against his mouth to suppress a wave of nausea.

Now he understood the reason for the salt pellets in the wall. Salt was a desiccant. The Nolands had used it to mummify their daughter's body so she could never be discovered. Which meant they could never sell their house for the risk of being found out. For years, they've pretended Sarah was still alive. No wonder no one had seen her.

John was disgusted, not by the appearance of the partially preserved body in front of him, but by the callus behavior of Ted and Mary-Beth Noland. How could parents behave in such a way? Their act was over. The Nolands would have to face the consequences of their actions. John would make sure of it.

He turned on his phone and scrolled down his call log until he found the number for Sheriff Thornsby. John dialed the number and listened to the ring tones, unable to take his eyes off Sarah, standing at attention in the nook of the wall like a toy soldier. The call kicked over to voice mail. John listened to Sheriff Thornsby's greeting, and after a tone beeped, he left a message.

"Sheriff, this is John Ferris. I found Sarah Noland. Please, come to the Nolands' house as soon as possible. It's an emergency."

He ended the call and slipped his cell phone into his pocket. He wondered whether he should continue tearing off drywall but decided that was the work for a forensic team. Who knows what kind of evidence they'd want to gather?

John's thoughts were interrupted by a noise from down-stairs: the sound of a door closing, footsteps, muffled voices. It was far too soon for the sheriff to be responding. He held his breath and listened intently.

He made out the voice of a man now. John recognized it as Ted Noland's voice. John had been too busy to notice that dusk was falling. It had gotten late in the day and the Nolands were back from Peoria.

John's pulse quickened as he cursed under his breath. What would he say to them if they found him snooping in their house? What did it matter? He had no explaining to do. They were the ones who needed to explain what the body of their daughter was doing buried in a wall of their home.

The best strategy was to remain upstairs and be quiet and hope the sheriff would arrive soon. As long as the Nolands stayed downstairs, he was safe.

John approached the door to the bedroom to be able to hear what was going on downstairs. He listened to the soft thud of a refrigerator closing, followed by the sound of liquid pouring into a glass. A television turned on to the nightly news.

Good, John thought. *Get comfortable and stay downstairs.* He wondered whether he should try to sneak out of the house but decided it would be too dangerous. He'd have to go down-stairs and cross the living room. They'd notice him for sure. Besides, he didn't want the Nolands to walk into Sarah's room and find a hole in the wall. They were crazy enough to move the body and hide all evidence of their wrongdoing before the sheriff got there. No. The best thing John could do was stay here with Sarah, never leaving her out of his sight.

A moment later John heard Ted cry out, "Why is there a breeze blowing through the living room?"

Mary-Beth answered meekly, "I don't know."

John knew. He hadn't shut the window through which he entered the house. He listened to the sound of heavy foot-steps, then Ted's voice. "Mary-Beth, did you leave the window in the den open?"

"No. I didn't," Mary-Beth replied.

"Well, it's open. And you're the only one who uses this room."

"I am telling you, I didn't open it."

"How many times do I have to tell you not to be so careless?"

Mary-Beth responded, "How many times do I have to tell you I didn't open it? I haven't opened that window in weeks."

What happened next made the hair stand up on John's neck. The conversation ended abruptly. The television cut off. The house descended in profound silence.

He knew what Ted and Mary-Beth were doing: they were listening for an intruder. They were listening for him.

Where the hell was the sheriff?

When John heard Ted and Mary-Beth whispering, he knew they were on to him. He tried to think what he'd say when they confronted him but was coming up blank.

There was a creak coming from the stairway. The Nolands were coming upstairs. John backed into Sarah's bedroom and waited.

A few moments later, Ted Noland filled the doorway. With a jeering voice, he said, "You! I should have known it was you."

John didn't say a word. He didn't have to. He simply pointed to Sarah's corpse peeking from the hole in the wall.

Ted Noland's eyes widened for just a moment. His face turned into a snarl. "You son of a bitch! I'll teach you to mind your own business." He lunged toward John and pointed something at him.

It wasn't a gun. John hadn't registered what the object Ted was holding was until he felt a wetness on his face, quickly followed by excruciating burning of his eyes and nose.

John screamed in pain. Ted got closer and sprayed his face again. John felt like his eyes were melting. He tried to rub his face on the front of his shirt with no relief. He writhed on the floor, blinded, trying to catch his breath.

That's when Ted landed the first punch. It caught John square on the jaw. The second fist landed on his already tender nose. John felt a kick in the ribs, another over his left kidney.

"You couldn't mind your own business, could you?" Ted said. "You had to pry into my family's affairs. Well, your days of snooping are over."

John lifted his arms in a gesture of self-protection. He opened his eyes a crack, the air rushing in like the heat of a furnace. His vision was fuzzy, but he could make out the form of Ted Noland lifting his arm to strike him. Another blur appeared in John's visual field. John blinked a few times and now saw it was Mary-Beth, standing behind her husband. She, too, had her hand held up in the air, and it came crashing onto Ted's head with a strange musical jingling sound.

Mary-Beth struck Ted again. John rubbed his eyes and was able to make out the weapon she had used: Sarah's toy piano. She hammered her husband again and again with feral wails until a familiar voice said, "That's enough. Drop it."

John blinked again and saw the towering form of Sheriff Thornsby in the doorway of the bedroom. Ted slumped to the floor, bleeding. Mary-Beth fell to her knees. She stared at the gap in the wall and began to cry.

"I'm sorry, baby. I'm so sorry, my little angel," she repeated.

The sheriff stepped inside the room, surveyed the scene, and said, "My dear Lord!"

Chapter Fifteen

The emergency room doctor was a young man in wrinkled scrubs who wore his stethoscope over his chest as if it was a medal.

"You doing okay there, John?" he asked in a condescending way.

John Ferris looked up at him from the hospital gurney and said, "I'm fine."

"I wouldn't say you're fine," the doctor said. "You have pretty severe contusions of the face. But you're lucky. Your facial x-rays show no fractures of the orbital sockets, maxilla, or mandible. And your corneas show no chemical burns from the pepper spray. So, yeah, you should have a complete recovery if you manage to stay out of trouble until you heal."

John had too many things on his mind to grab the doctor by the neck. He limited himself to asking, "Can I go home now?"

The doctor said, "Your nurse is working on your discharge paperwork. But the sheriff asked us to keep you until after he has had a word with you." The doctor winked and said, "Catch you next time," and walked out of the room. *The little prick.*

John tried sitting up in bed but felt a little lightheaded. He lay down again, closed his eyes, and let out a long slow exhalation. What he needed was some rest. When was the last time he had had a whole night's sleep?

A minute later, he heard footsteps and a soft grunt. John opened his eyes and saw Sheriff Brad Thornsby standing over the gurney.

The sheriff said, "Are you hanging in there, partner?"

John sat up and said, "I'm fine. Just a little beat."

"I can see that," the sheriff said. "The doctor informed me you're ready for discharge. I figured maybe you could use a ride home."

"I would really appreciate that, sheriff. More than you would know."

The sheriff nodded. "My pleasure. It'll give us time to chat."

A nurse stepped into the room with a stack of papers and a pen. The sheriff said, "I'll wait for you in the hallway." He tipped his hat at the nurse and ambled out of the room.

The nurse had John sign a few documents, handed him a prescription for painkillers, and asked him if he needed help getting into his street clothes.

"I can manage," John said.

Ten minutes later, he was getting into the front passenger seat of Sheriff Thornsby's patrol car.

After he pulled out of the hospital's parking lot, the sheriff said, "What a day, huh?"

John didn't say anything for a while. When they stopped at a red light, he asked, "What will happen to the Nolands?"

"They'll remain in custody pending complete psychiatric evaluations. From the looks of it, Ted will be committed to an institution. The doctor's initial assessment is that he's suffering from a complete psychotic break. Mary-Beth is exhibiting symptoms more consistent with post-traumatic stress disorder. Then we'll have to wait and see what the district attorney's office will decide as far as criminal charges."

"Sarah's death was an accident," John said.

The light turned green. The sheriff slowly throttled the gas pedal and said, "That's what Mary-Beth claims. All the same, failure to properly dispose of a human body is a felony, punishable by up to ten years in prison."

"I don't think it was Mary-Beth's fault. I think Ted forced her to do it," John said. "She had no choice but to go along."

"I think you're probably right about that," the sheriff said. "Judging by how she smashed that toy piano on his head today. You know, a woman can take only so much before she says, 'Enough!' I reckon Mary-Beth has suffered enough. But, as I said, it's up to the prosecutor's discretion."

"And Sarah?" John asked.

"She'll get a proper burial," Sheriff Thornsby said. "I'll make sure of that."

"Thank you, sheriff."

"I should thank you, Mr. Ferris. And I should apologize. Things might have worked out better had I listened to you."

John shook his head. "The whole story is so hard to believe. Their daughter dies, and they act as if she's still alive for five years."

"And no one would have been the wiser if you hadn't moved next door," the sheriff said. "What I can't figure out is how did you know?"

"How did I know what?"

"How did you know the girl was deceased?" the sheriff asked.

"Well, I didn't."

"Why'd you break into their house today? Don't worry. You're not going to be prosecuted for your actions. I'm just trying to figure it all out."

John took a deep breath. "I wanted to find her."

"So, you thought she was alive. But you punched a hole in their wall. What on earth made you do that?"

John said, "By that point, I knew she was dead."

"What changed your mind?"

John hesitated to reply. "I had a vision."

"A vision? What kind of vision?"

"Sheriff, I can't explain it. I can't explain much of what has happened since I came to this town."

"Fair enough," the sheriff said. He took the ramp off the highway and turned right onto Maple Park's main street.

"What about your reports of the little girl running into your yard at night?" the sheriff asked.

"I guess that was all in my head, too."

"Okay. What about the rock through the window? That sure as heck wasn't in your head."

John covered his face with his hands. "I don't know, sheriff. I just don't know."

The sheriff groaned as he turned into John's street. "You've been through a lot. That's for sure. If there's anything else you want to tell me, I promise to keep it between the two of us."

John placed his hands on his knees. He said, "There is one thing, actually."

"I'm all ears," the sheriff said as he pulled into John's parkway and put the gear shifter in park.

"Come inside," John said. "I have to show you something."

Chapter Sixteen

"Would you like some coffee?" John asked Sheriff Thornsby. The officer shook his head. John invited Brad Thornsby to sit at the kitchen table and went to his bedroom. His infrared digital camera was sitting on the bedside table.

John returned to the kitchen and sat across from the sheriff, the camera in his hands. He said, "The night the Nolands reported me to your office, the night Mary-Beth accused me of being a peeping Tom, I took some photographs of my backyard. It was pitch-black outside. I couldn't see anything with the naked eye. But I used an infrared light source, a light for a security system, and this is a special camera with a filter removed. It's able to take pictures of infrared light."

The sheriff brought his hands together on the table. "Mr. Ferris, why were you taking pictures of your yard at night?"

"I thought I'd catch Sarah in the act, have proof that she was pestering me," John said.

"With an infrared camera?"

"That's right," John said with a tinge of embarrassment. "Anyway, while I was waiting, I decided to take a few shots, you know, to test the camera. That's when Mary-Beth spotted me, and all the trouble started. But later that evening, I took a look at the snapshots I had taken. They showed nothing of particular interest. Except for one picture, which had a flash of light in the middle, a blur, really. I figured I might have caught a strange reflection, or maybe a bug flew right in front of the lens as I snapped the picture."

"Sounds reasonable," the sheriff said.

"But I took a second look a couple of days later, and the photograph had changed. I can't explain it. The flair of light had retracted, and a shape was barely visible behind it."

The sheriff pursed his lips and sat pensively for a few moments. "How do you explain that?"

"I can't explain it," John said. "That's the problem."

The sheriff nodded. "Mr. Ferris, I'm going to ask you a question, and I want you to be straight with me. I promise I'll keep your answer confidential, and this will be the last time I'll bring up the subject."

"What do you want to know?" John asked.

Sheriff Thornsby locked eyes with John and said, "Mr. Ferris, did you throw that rock through your bedroom window?"

"No. I swear. I was in bed. You saw how the glass fell inside on the bedroom floor. The rock had to be thrown from outside."

"I'm sorry for asking, but I have to be sure you didn't do it."

"Sheriff, you have to believe me."

The sheriff nodded. "I'm guessing you want to show me that picture you took."

John's palms were growing sweaty. He placed the camera on the table and rubbed his hands together. "I'm almost scared to look," John said.

The sheriff leaned over the table. "Show me."

John took the camera in his hands, held it at an angle so both men could view the screen, and pressed the power button. When the screen lit up, Sheriff Thornsby muttered, "Holy Mary and Joseph." His jaw dropped, unable to take his eyes off the screen.

Both men studied the photograph, which showed John's backyard, with a vertical bar of light in the foreground, like a stretched halo, less prominent than the last time John had viewed it. Behind the veil of light, they made out a little girl walking through the yard in what appeared to be a summer dress.

After a long silence, the sheriff said, "How is this possible?"

"I don't know," John said. "I was hoping you could explain it."

The sheriff looked away and rubbed his jaw. He waited a moment before asking John, "Has anyone else seen this photograph?"

John shook his head. "Just you and me."

"Delete it," the sheriff said.

"What?"

"You have to delete it. And never mention a word of it to anyone. Some things are best left unspoken."

John said, "No one would believe me anyway."

"I hardly believe it, and I saw it with my own eyes," the sheriff said.

"You're right. It's time to let Sarah rest in peace." John pressed a button on the camera, scrolled down a menu of options on the screen, and selected 'delete.' He pushed the power button and placed the camera on the table.

The sheriff leaned back in his chair and crossed his arms. After waiting for a beat, he said, "You wouldn't have something stronger than coffee to drink, would you?"

Chapter Seventeen

The interment of Sarah Noland took place on a cold sunny afternoon in early December. A slight breeze blew from the northeast, bringing with it the smell of dry hay and burning wood.

Few people attended the somber graveside ceremony. Mary-Beth Noland was accompanied by a county-appointed social worker and her mother, who had driven from Peoria early that morning. Sheriff Brad Thornsby was there, flanked by his deputy, Frank Billing. John Ferris followed the service from a respectful distance in the company of his colleague, Brenda Collins. Ted Noland was conspicuously absent. He was being detained in the psychiatric ward of a hospital in DeKalb, awaiting the criminal court's determination on whether he was competent to stand trial.

The service was short, but the words of the presiding pastor were heartfelt and profound. Everyone in attendance was moved by the solemnity of the moment when the small pearl-white casket was slowly lowered into the earth.

John whispered, "Goodbye, Sarah. Rest in peace."

When the service ended, John felt a compelling urge to express his sentiments of sorrow to his former neighbor. He approached Mary-Beth and said, "Mrs. Noland, I wanted to extend my sincere condolences. I'm so sorry for your loss."

Mary-Beth looked at John with swollen, blood-shot eyes. She asked her social worker, a morose plump woman with librarian glasses if she could have a moment alone to talk to John. The social worker nodded and stepped away, clutching the arm of Mary-Beth's mother.

Mary-Beth looked down and said, "Mr. Ferris, I wanted to apologize for how I treated you. I'm sorry I shouted at you and called the police."

"Mary-Beth, there's no need to apologize," John said.

"I know you must have found my behavior unacceptable, even bizarre, but when you moved in next doors, Ted's behavior became increasingly erratic. He was growing more paranoid by the day. He thought you were out to get him. At one point, he convinced himself you might be an undercover FBI agent. The more paranoid he became, the more abusive he was toward me. He'd threaten me and beat me. He accused me of being in cahoots with you. I had to prove my allegiance to him for my own safety. So, I yelled at you. I tried to do what I could to keep you away. When I called the sheriff's department, I did it to protect you. He was going to kill you that night. It was only the arrival of the sheriff that thwarted his plan." Tears streamed down Mary-Beth's face.

John took her hand and said, "Mary-Beth, I can't imagine what you had to endure. I hope you find a way to overcome your pain."

"Thank you, Mr. Ferris. Thank you for finding Sarah. Thank you for making this day possible. Can I ask you one last favor?"

The way Mary-Beth looked at him broke John's heart. "Of course," he said.

"Please, don't forget my little Sarah. She was such a cheerful little girl. You would have liked her, and she would have loved you. Keep her alive in your heart. And from time to time, say a little prayer for her."

"I'll do that, Mary-Beth. I promise you. I'll do what I can to keep Sarah's memory alive."

Chapter Eighteen

Two years later . . .

John Ferris stood up from the hard plastic chair and began pacing the hospital waiting room. He stuffed his hands into his pockets and looked out the windows that opened onto the Chicago skyline. Beyond the city spread the shimmering expanse of Lake Michigan.

A television mounted in the waiting room corner played the evening news broadcast. To John, it was little more than background noise until a story made his ears perk.

The news anchor had mentioned the name Ted Noland. It made John spin on his heels. He listened intently to the most recent update on the sordid story of a husband and wife who hid the body of their dead daughter behind the wall of the girl's bedroom. The reporter's summary of the case seemed to be missing something. The facts of the story were accurate but came across as devoid of meaning.

How could they know the significance of the events? They weren't there to see what John had seen. And if they had been there, they would have hardly believed their eyes. Nonetheless, news of the events spread like wildfire and became regular fodder for national news outlets and gossip magazines.

John Ferris had spent many an hour reliving those days in Maple Park in his mind. After a great deal of reflection, he had reached an inexorable conclusion.

Sarah Noland had died years before in a tragic accident. But her soul lived on in limbo, unable to move on. The girl's spirit was not trapped by torment but by love. She loved her parents and saw how they suffered her loss, how they carried on as though she were still alive, unable to move on with their own lives. It was only with John exposing the morbid secret that Ted and Mary-Beth Noland were forced to face reality and accept the consequences of their actions.

Mary-Beth had made significant progress. She lived in a halfway house and volunteered at a shelter for runaway teenagers. She was slowly coming to terms with her past.

Ted Noland, on the other hand, lost all grips with reality. As the news anchor now reported, he was committed to an institution for the criminally insane, where he still maintained his daughter was very much alive.

John Ferris reached up and turned off the television set. He was about to settle back into the stiff hospital chair of the empty waiting room when a nurse stepped in and called his name.

"Mr. Ferris? Please follow me."

John Ferris stiffened. "Is everything okay?"

"Your wife is resting in the recovery room. She had something called placenta previa. She lost quite a bit of blood, but the Cesarean section was a success. She'll be fine."

"What about . . ." John's voice trailed off. He was too frightened to mouth the words.

The nurse smiled. "The baby is fine. Are you ready to meet your daughter, Mr. Ferris?"

John thought his knees might crumple under him. He placed his hand over his mouth as his eyes welled with tears and managed to nod.

"Follow me, Mr. Ferris," the nurse said.

She brought him to the vestibule of the hospital nursery, where she asked John to don a disposable paper gown and wash his hands with antiseptic soap in a large stainless steel sink. He toweled off his hands and followed the nurse into a room, his knees stiff, his steps shaky.

As John settled into a plush couch, another nurse wheeled a bassinet into the room. She lifted a rolled-up bundle and placed it into John's waiting arms.

The nurse said, "Say hello to your baby girl."

John cradled the infant in his arms and gazed at her features, her plump cheeks, pouty lips, upturned nose, and gray-blue eyes that looked at him inquisitively. John chuckled when the baby opened her mouth and stuck her little tongue out at him.

The nurse said, "She's a precious one."

"She's amazing," John said.

"Your first one?"

"Yes."

"Well, I'll tell you one thing. Your life will never be the same."

"I know," John said. "Yes, I know." As John gaped at his daughter, he wondered how he had ever been able to live without her. Yes, his life would never be the same. And he was overjoyed by the realization.

"Have you and your wife picked a name?" the nurse asked him.

"We have." He looked at the nurse brimming with pride and said, "Her name is Sarah."

About The Author

Faraz Ahmed is a Zend Certified PHP Web Developer, Writer, and CBT Life Coach from Karachi, Pakistan, and the Top Rated+ Freelancer on Upwork. He loves writing technical help books and mystery, horror, and sci-fi stories.

To find out more about Faraz Ahmed, please visit www.farazthewebguy.com

Other Books By Faraz Ahmed

Top Secrets of Becoming a Successful Freelance Web Developer

https://www.amazon.com/dp/B098TNDBGX/